A TINY SPARK

Elite House Publishing, LLC
Lafayette, Indiana

This is a work of fiction. Any similarity to actual persons, living or dead, or actual events, is purely coincidental.

Cover photo © Edoma/Shutterstock.com

Book Design by Karina Granda

ISBN 979-8-9854262-0-5 (Hardcover)
ISBN 979-8-9854262-1-2 (Paperback)
ISBN 979-8-9854262-2-9 (eBook)

A TINY SPARK

Brittney Kreighbaum

ELITE

Lafayette, Indiana

Chapter **One**

I REACHED ACROSS THE BAR, SLIDING THE DRAFT beer to one of my usuals. I saw him staring at me, his eyebrows pulled together. He reached up with one hand to rub his chin like he was thinking of what to say before shaking his head to himself. I followed his gaze down my chest to see what had caught his eye. My apron had slid down exposing the large bruise above my right breast which my maroon V-neck failed to cover. I quickly rearranged the apron and gave him a reassuring smile. Would he mention it to my boss? I prayed not. It wasn't the first time I had come to work with a bruise, but they were getting harder and harder to cover up. I didn't want any questions. How far would Austin go if someone found out? If I told the truth, he would surely kill me like he had promised so many times.

Austin Pierce was the only one I had left since my parents died three years ago. Most of my friends graduated high school and left our small town. With only 1,463 people, it was a cozy place to live from the outside looking in. Austin and I had been together since I was nineteen, which made it two and a half years now. He slapped me in the face once at the beginning of our relationship, but it was an accident and he apologized profusely for days after it happened. I could tell he was shocked at his own actions in the heat of the moment as he froze, his jaw falling apart before he began to apologize. I believed him when he said it was a mistake as he didn't raise a hand to me for a long time after that, until I moved in with him.

It didn't take long for him to become controlling and obsessive. He regularly went through my phone. I tried to stand up to him about it last night and that's when he punched me in the chest. Just the one hit made my breath catch in my throat and regret flood through my mind. I had kept my distance from Austin the rest of the night. But if my boss found out, he would try to intervene or something. I'm sure it would be with good intentions, but it would only make things worse for me.

I kept my eye on the customer all night, making sure I was the one to order his drinks so he wouldn't have a chance to talk to anybody else. At the end of my shift, he was still there, but much too hammered on whiskey to remember anything about a bruise he saw on his bartender's chest. I clocked out, changing into my jacket to walk home.

It was a short walk and my body became more tense with every step, as I approached the house. I paused outside the front door, taking a deep breath. I had no idea what kind of mood Austin would be in when I walked through the door. His mood was always unpredictable. Most of the time I didn't even know what I did to make him angry or constantly accuse me of cheating. I was getting better at assessing his disposition, but nothing ever prepared me for the seemingly endless anger he had stored up inside him. Sometimes, it felt like he hated me.

Austin was sitting in the living room watching TV. As I threw my shoes to the side of the breezeway, I immediately assessed the hard features of his face: the tight line of his mouth, his flared nostrils, the rigid hunch of his shoulders. He was ready for a fight.

"I'm home," I called, as I rushed up the stairs, trying to buy myself a head start.

He didn't respond, but I heard him coming up the stairs heavy-footed as I grabbed a towel to shower. As I shut the closet door, he grabbed ahold of my ponytail, yanking me toward him. The force of his pull lit my scalp on fire.

"Why are you late?" he snapped. "Where the hell were you?"

"I was at the bar, working," I replied, attempting to pull my hair away from him. And even though I knew contradicting him would only make him angrier, I added, "I'm not late, Austin, I got off ten minutes ago and walked home."

"From now on, you call me when you leave," he said, shoving me toward the bathroom. "Go shower. You smell like smoke and booze."

I didn't say anything in response; it was easier—*safer*—to just do as he said. Taking an extremely long shower in hopes of him falling asleep worked most of the time. By the time I finished, he was passed out in the bed we shared. Silently, I changed into my pajamas, pausing at the foot of the bed. I quietly grabbed my pillow and headed downstairs to the couch.

As I settled into the deep cushions and pulled the scratchy throw blanket over me, the only sound through the entire house was Austin snoring, faintly, upstairs. I was so exhausted from the long day, but as I laid there I couldn't sleep. This sick, nagging pit was growing inside of me. I was starting to feel less loved and more like a piece of property, losing myself day by day.

The next morning, I woke up as ice-cold water splashed all over me. I flung myself from the couch, looking around. Austin was standing over me, an empty pitcher in his hand.

"What the hell, Austin!" I shouted, instantly realizing the mistake I had just made.

He threw the pitcher at me. "Why the fuck are you sleeping on the couch?"

"The bedroom was too hot last night," I stammered. "It was cooler down here."

He saw right through my lie. His lips pulled back to bare his teeth as he charged me like a bull. I covered my face with my arms, only to feel the sting of his punch in my stomach. When I reached for my belly, he slapped me in the face. My eyes stung with tears as he grabbed my chin, forcing me to meet his angry stare.

"There better not be someone else, Noelle," he threatened, "or I *will* kill you."

"There's not," I muttered.

He shoved me backward, walking into the kitchen. "Clean that shit up. The couch better not be ruined because of your dumb ass."

I looked at the soaked couch cushions. As I was trying to dry them with a towel, he slammed the front door behind him, leaving for work. I couldn't hold it in any longer. It was hard enough I had to walk on eggshells, but when he found every way to make my life feel like a prison, I hated myself for allowing it. Why did he accuse me of cheating? I did anything he asked and only went from home to work and back. I had cut off all my friendships except one. What else did I have to do for this torment to stop? I desperately wanted things to go back to the way they were before we moved in together.

I went for a run before my shift at the bar. Running cleared my head and was my escape. It also was a workout I needed, as I was told repeatedly by Austin. It helped me release all the built-up emotions I couldn't express without fear of him getting angry.

I jumped the fence to run the trails through the woods, stopping when I got to the clearing by the waterfall. This was where my parents had first met when they were young. I liked to talk to them there—figuratively, of course.

"All right, Mom...Dad, what do I do? I need to get out of this situation," I started to feel more tears coming. "I can't live like this. Give me a sign or something. I don't think I can do this on my own. I need help." I waited. Of course, nothing actually happened, but I was more hopeful that maybe something would come to me.

I pulled myself together and started my run back toward town, stopping to get a coffee like I always did. Alex, my regular barista, smiled at me as she got my usual ready.

"You know, Noelle, you should really reopen your mom's bookstore across the street," she said. "Out-of-towners come in all the time and ask if it's open. You could even rent out the apartment above it. I might know someone, if you are interested."

I smiled at the idea. "I just might. My mom loved that store. She used to say it was her purpose to give people the power to live a thousand lives."

"A thousand lives?" Her brows furrowed.

"Yeah. She would say when you read a book it's like living another life through a character in the book. It's a quote from someone, I'm sure. She always spouted quotes at everyone."

"Ah, that makes sense." She slid my coffee toward me. "It would be nice to look across the street and see the store thriving again."

"I think it thrived because people liked to stop in there to talk books and authors for hours on end," I smiled, heading for the door. "I will most definitely give it some thought."

Was this my sign? Open the bookstore again? I thought about it all day. Throughout my shift at the bar, I found myself distracted as I pondered what to do. I talked to my boss about it. He was behind me all the way. He even offered to help me clean it up. So did the other bartender. By the time I got home, I wanted to tell Austin about it, too. My decision wasn't final, but I was warming up to the idea of doing something my mom had done. But before I got one word out, he had me pinned against the wall.

"What the hell did I tell you yesterday?" he shouted, an inch from my face.

What did he say? I was trying to remember as he tightened his grip on my throat.

"I said call me when you leave the bar...and you didn't. Why do you disobey me, Noelle?" he snapped. I tried to push him away as it got harder to breathe.

"St—stop, Austin. I—I can't—"

He threw me to the floor. I coughed, gasping for air. He kicked me in the side once before pulling me back to my feet by my hair. He dragged me into the kitchen, my feet tripping over one another. He grabbed a small knife and showed it to me. I froze. Was he going to kill me? He ran it across the top of my arm, just pressing hard enough to slice my skin. I screamed. My arm burned as blood dripped onto the counter. He threw the knife in the sink.

"Now, this will help you remember to call, won't it, you stupid bitch?"

I nodded.

"Go clean yourself up and stop fucking crying before you really make me angry."

I ran upstairs to the bathroom, locked the door behind me, and fell to the floor. I started the shower so he wouldn't hear me cry. I looked at myself in the mirror, arm bloodied and face puffy. What was happening to me? This was not the life I wanted. I had to get out, but how? I knew Austin wouldn't just let me end it. I remembered what my barista said this morning—*you could even rent out the apartment above it.* Maybe I wouldn't rent it. Maybe it could be my own place. I could move my stuff in little by little without him knowing.

During the period between my parents' deaths and moving in with Austin, I'd lived in the small apartment by myself. Most of my furniture and belongings were still there since Austin only allowed me to bring my clothes, some favorite books, and pictures of my parents. I didn't own much in the house at all. This meant I could just leave and not come back. It sounded like my best option.

The next day I repeated my routine, except instead of going to my shift at the bar, my boss, William, and I started the clean-up at the store. I took a few pieces of clothing over to the apartment. I also got the power turned on and in my name. William helped me change the locks—updated locks meant Austin wouldn't have a key. Then I called at the normal time to let him know I was on my way home. Everything was calm when I got there, but I had to take the risk of telling him about the bookstore.

"That's great," he said, smiling at me. "If you need extra help, let me know, babe."

I was immediately confused by his supportive attitude. He pulled me toward him, kissing my cheek. I was waiting for a punch or something. When nothing came, I looked at him.

He sighed. "Noelle, I'm sorry I've been on edge these past couple days. I was just really stressed out at work and took it out on you."

My heart broke in half from sheer guilt. I could tell he was being genuine and here I was, trying to leave him behind his back. Maybe it would all get better from here on out. Maybe he was sorry and wouldn't do it again. I could just open the bookstore like normal. I didn't *have* to move my stuff out little by little. I decided to see how it all played out. I hoped he was truthful and it would never happen again.

All week, William and I worked on the store. Austin was uncharacteristically kind. He took two days off from work to ensure I'd be able to open it by that Saturday. He took on the job of setting up a few bookshelves when I got the shipment in and even brought me plants for the front entrance from a store in the city. Once again, the guilt hit me like a ton of bricks. He was helping me clean and prepare the store, yet the plan was to leave him once it had opened? As it started to eat away at me inside, I found myself going the extra mile to do things for him. Each day, I made dinner for him and kept the house clean the way he liked. I'd even gone so far as to do his laundry. The question of whether this was a turning point for us or just a period of dormancy for his angry side, sat in the back of my mind.

The bar was always packed on Fridays, and tonight was no different. With all the help William and Austin had contributed, I was ready to open the store the next morning, so I kept my shift at the bar to help. By ten o'clock, the bar was packed. We normally got a rush of people from the city on the weekends due to the lake on the other side of town, a great spot for fishing and bonfires. I made a ton in tips on these nights. But tonight, there was something different. I noticed it when two guys came in and sat in my section. It seemed like people were staring at them, glancing over their shoulders and whispering behind their hands as they walked through the bar. They were good-looking for sure, both with jet-black hair and wearing black T-shirts revealing toned arms. But something told me that wasn't the only reason people were taking notice.

In recent weeks, I had heard rumors about a mafia connection in town, but in our small town, who knew if that was accurate? One person could have said something about knowing a guy in the mafia and by the time it got around, that same person was the head of that same mafia! Gossip was simply a form of free entertainment for the residents of this town. So, these two were the so-called mobsters, I gathered.

"What can I get you to drink?" I asked them, with a smile.

"Whatever you have on tap, two."

I turned quickly to fill their order. As I slid their beers toward them, I noticed a tattoo across each of their forearms that read *Poca favilla gran fiamma seconda.* I paused, surprised. Why was that phrase important to them? I stood there, lost in thought.

"Oh, sorry," one said, as he slid two five-dollar bills across the bar top.

I shook my head, sliding them back. "No, I've never met someone with the same tattoo as me—let alone two of you."

"Let me guess, you think it means love and peace in Italian?" The other one spoke, crossing his arms over his chest, leaning back in his chair, and rolling his eyes at me. He'd made his voice higher-pitched as he said the words 'love' and 'peace' as though he was trying to imitate a woman's voice.

"Damon, don't be rude," the other one said.

I snorted, pulling back the collar of my shirt to reveal my tattoo of the saying inked just below my collarbone, never breaking eye contact as I recited the quote—"*A mighty flame followeth a tiny spark.*"

He sat up, his arms falling from where they were across his chest. His eyebrows rose on his forehead, his mouth parting slightly. This sight of him gave me such satisfaction I smiled to myself.

"But if you think yours means, how did you say it, *love and peace*, you might want to get it translated," I taunted.

Walking away, I heard the other guy laughing. "That's a first."

I had no idea what had just come over me. The Noelle I was now, courtesy of Austin and his unrelenting abuse, would never speak out to anyone. For that moment, I remembered my old, more carefree self. The one that spoke her mind confidently and wasn't afraid of a fight. My heart ached a bit as I remembered her, wanting her to stay. But that would be impossible as long as I was with Austin.

It only got busier throughout the night. I checked in on the two guys periodically but they had soon just become two more orders to fill in the blur of drink requests I was getting as the night progressed. Finally getting a break, I sat at the back table in the corner. I made the mistake of checking my messages, all from Austin. The texts were just as horrible as what he said to me in person. It was deflating that the kind version of him only lasted long enough to get the store ready. I read the first two, saying what a waste of space I am and how stupid I was. Before I knew it, I was getting visibly upset. I felt my eyes water as tears threatened to spill down my cheeks. I was looking toward the ceiling to get them to stop when the two guys sat across from me.

"Everything okay?" the sarcastic one asked.

I quickly recovered, wiping my eyes, taking a breath. "Sorry guys, I'm on break."

"It will only take a minute."

I nodded, waiting for them to speak.

"I'm Giovanni, this is Damon. We just moved here from the city. Don't take offense, but what else is there to do here besides hanging out at this bar?"

I laughed slightly. "Noelle, and none taken. Well, we have the bar, the trails, and the square. I'm sorry to say, that is about it."

"Can you elaborate?"

"The square is about a five-minute walk from here. It has all the little shops and restaurants. At the end of the road, there is a park where there are cookouts and things during the summer. There are trails to hike or run. They lead to a clearing with a water-fall. They're fenced off, courtesy of the local police department, but if you're into breaking the law, it's worth it. Other than that, I sug-gest you venture back to the city."

"You sound like you jump the fence often," Damon said, his slate gray eyes giving me a mischievous look. "Ever gotten caught?"

"I run every morning, and I got caught once...but never again," I smiled slyly.

He smiled with me, revealing his perfect teeth and dimpled

cheeks. What was happening to me? I felt brave—bolder than I've been in a long time—just by their presence.

"Your arm is bleeding," Giovanni pointed out.

I looked down to see Austin's cut bleeding through the bandage. I must have hit it on something. I peeled back the bandages, wincing as they came off. I quickly realized that I needed to clean up my arm, so I excused myself and went to the bathroom to replace them. When I came back, they were still sitting there.

"What happened? That looked like a pretty nasty cut," Damon asked.

"I'm just clumsy. It's not a big deal," I attempted to reassure them, as I sat back down.

It wasn't much longer before the other bartender, Madison, came over to the table. She handed me a list of drinks.

"My turn for a break, I need a smoke. Here are the orders from the bar top."

I was glad there was no time for more questions. I smiled toward them. "Break's over, but if you have any other questions, you know where I'll be."

As I started the other half of my shift, time dragged on. I was in the middle of filling drinks when Austin came in. He screamed my name over the music. I jumped out of my skin, and then locked over. His eyes were bloodshot, his jaw tightly clenched to match his fists at his sides. I was sure he wouldn't do anything in front of people so I walked over to him. But when he grabbed me by the arm and walked me outside, I knew I was in for it. A tight, heavy ball formed in the pit of my stomach as I began to rethink the day. What could I have done to make him this angry?

"You were supposed to be home thirty minutes ago, why are you still here?"

"It's busy. I have to stay until close tonight."

He backhanded me once, my cheek burning in an instant. "I got home and dinner wasn't ready, you weren't home yet, and the house was a mess."

He hit me again, this time in the nose. The taste of blood filled my mouth. He punched me in the side; his knuckles against my rib cage knocked the wind out of me. I fell to the ground, my hands barely holding me up. He kicked my stomach twice.

"Useless piece of shit!" he screamed, pulling me to my feet with a fistful of my hair.

"I'm sorry," I cried. "It won't happen again. I'm sorry!"

"Next time you call me for permission to stay, got it?"

I nodded, apologizing once more. My face was hot from the sting of his slap.

"You better bring home good tips to make this up to me," he spat as he shoved me toward the door.

I ran inside just as Madison was coming out from the kitchen.

"What happened?" she asked, running up to inspect my face.

"An angry customer. I cut him off, he got mad." I tried to recover, wiping a tear from my cheek.

"Here." She pulled her towel from her back pocket. "It's not the cleanest, but it'll do the job until we get you in back."

I walked back toward the bar. William came to talk to me,

making sure I was okay, asking me if he should call the police. Before I got to the back room, I heard someone call my name. When I turned, I saw Damon and Giovanni. I wiped my nose with the towel before giving them my attention.

"Are you okay?" Damon asked, reaching out for me before stopping himself.

"Yeah, just an angry customer. He's an out-of-towner, I'm fine, really."

"He hit you?" he asked, beginning to scan the room in search of the culprit. "Where is he?"

I smiled, more genuine, "I appreciate it, but it's nothing. Just enjoy your night, guys."

He started to say something in protest, but Giovanni quickly cut him off, speaking in another language. I recognized it as Italian but I didn't understand what he was saying. Damon then smiled, holding out his hand. I took it, shaking it.

"I'll see you around, Noelle."

I nodded, getting back to cleaning up my face. When I came back out customers were staring at me. It started to clear out over the next hour, which made me feel less anxious. I was relieved when the last customer left and we started our closing duties. After we counted down the register, I called Austin to let him know I was on my way. He didn't answer, so I left a message to cover my bases.

My nerves were on high alert by the time I got home. I felt all my muscles relax as I came upon him passed out in bed. I thought about sleeping on the couch again, but I didn't want a repeat of the other morning's ice water wake-up call. I quickly showered in the dark so I didn't wake him with the lights, and crawled into bed. I felt him move and I flinched, covering my face, thinking he was going to hit me again. But instead, he reached his arm around me and kissed my head.

"Good night, Noelle, sweet dreams."

I was speechless. Did he mean what he said about trying to change? I couldn't handle the rollercoaster of emotions I felt every time I walked through the front door. After catching a glimpse of the old me come out at the bar tonight, I really missed my life before Austin. The burden of having to sleep with one eye open was not easy. I tossed and turned, wrestling with the thoughts of my old self. The last time I looked at the clock it was four A.M.

Chapter **Two**

THE NEXT MORNING, I WOKE UP TO THE SMELL OF eggs and coffee. I walked down the stairs, ready for anything. Austin was in the kitchen when I entered.

"Good morning, I made breakfast," he said, his voice full and bright. "I woke up starving!"

I looked around at all the food as he handed me a full plate. We sat down at the kitchen table and ate breakfast together. This was something we had never done before in all the time we'd been together. I didn't say anything because, well...I didn't know what to say. I didn't want to set him off again. I sat there, growing more confused, not understanding what this unprecedented gesture meant. Before I knew it, he was done with his breakfast, had washed the dishes, gotten ready for work, and was kissing me goodbye on his way out the door. I sat in my chair for ten minutes trying to figure out if this was a test or not. If it was, I had better stick to my normal routine. So, I got my gear on and headed for the trails for a run.

When I got to the clearing, I took my shirt off, letting the sun hit my exposed skin. My sports bra pressed against my bruises both new and old. It pinched a little, but the run was worth it. The shoe-sized bruise on my ribs was dark purple and hurt when I twisted my upper body. I was wiping the sweat off my face with my shirt when I heard footfalls on the trail coming through the trees.

"Hey, oh sorry." It was Damon and Giovanni.

They had on workout shorts and T-shirts. They'd taken my advice on running the trails. The beads of sweat glistened on them, reflecting those on my own skin. Skin that was bruised and was, I suddenly realized, exposed to them.

"Sorry, I didn't mean to make you uncomfortable. No one else usually comes up here this early in the morning." I quickly put my shirt back on, so they wouldn't see the bruise.

"Uncomfortable, no—you're just—"

"Think before you speak," Giovanni whispered.

Damon paused. "You're in pretty good shape?"

It sounded more like a question as he was trying to avoid saying what he really wanted to say. I couldn't help but giggle as Giovanni smacked his hand to his forehead.

"*That's* what you came up with?" he asked.

Damon scratched his head. "Yeah...that was it."

"It's not a big deal," I reassured them. "Really it's not."

"The trails are great by the way, thanks for the tip," Giovanni smiled, trying to get back on track to a normal conversation.

"No problem, you should also try the coffee shop," I turned and pointed to the nearest trailhead. "If you run down this trail, it will lead you right to it."

"Do you go that way?" Damon asked.

"Why do you want to know?" I teased.

"No reason, I was just wondering." He blushed.

"I go that way every morning. Alex, the barista, will have my coffee ready in about five minutes," I explained looking at my watch. "Which means I need to start heading that way. I'll see you guys around."

They waved as I headed back down the trail.

I stopped in to grab my morning cup of coffee and then headed home to get ready. I put on my favorite outfit that Austin approved of, taking extra time to do my hair. I stood in front of my closet after getting ready, debating on bringing more clothes to the apartment.

He'd been kind all week, but what happened at the bar the night before pushed me to continue with my plan, just in case. Sure, this morning was nice, but what would it be like when he came home, or tomorrow morning? I packed a small backpack with clothes I wasn't allowed to wear. A black mini skirt that Austin said made me look like a prostitute. The backless green halter top that I'd only worn once before he tried to rip it from my body, claiming I only wore it to attract the attention of other men. My favorite wine red sleeveless bodycon dress with cut outs on the sides to reveal parts of my torso. He didn't even let me wear it before he tried to throw it in the fire he had out back one night, calling me a slut for even buying it in the first place. My thought was that he wouldn't notice they were gone, as they'd been stashed so he wouldn't throw them away.

When I started down the sidewalk, a giddiness took hold of me. I was reclaiming not only my clothes, but my life. A smile sprouted on my lips at the thought of opening the store for the first time in many years.

By the time I got there, it was eleven a.m. I looked at the store-front from the sidewalk. *All right, here we go,* I thought to myself as I walked inside and flipped the closed sign to open. I wasn't expecting any customers right away, but heard the bell above the door ring only ten minutes after I opened. I glanced up from the book I was reading. It was Alex from across the street.

"You're open!" she shrieked, "I'll send customers over to you." She glanced around, "Wow, you kept everything almost the same. I remember coming in here with my mom when I was a kid. She would always let me pick one book, and then I would have to bring one book in to donate."

I nodded. "I was in charge of putting books away. I remember my mom letting me sit on the counter when customers weren't here," I told her. "I even got to ring a sale up once. She took care of the money, of course, but I got to scan the book. I was so excited to hear that beeping noise."

We both laughed as we continued reminiscing through her entire break. After she left, the store was quiet again, but only for a few minutes. Customers began walking from the coffee shop to my store, drinks in hand. I made a mental note to thank her in some way for all the customers. It was steady business for the rest of the day, and I didn't even get a chance to restock the shelves. I figured I would do that after I closed the store. I just had to remember to let Austin know.

Damon came in right before I closed. He was so absorbed in his phone he didn't even look up. I waited patiently as he walked through the aisles of books. Walking toward me, still looking at his phone, he started to speak.

"You don't have any Dante, do y—Noelle?" he looked confused. "You work here, too?"

"This, I own. It was my parent's. Well, my mom was in charge of it. I just reopened today, actually." I smiled.

He leaned on the counter. "So, you like to read?"

"I do," I said. "You can escape into books in a way that you can't in reality."

"A reader lives a thousand lives."

My jaw dropped. "My mom used to say that all the time! Well, she'd say it was her purpose: to give people the opportunity to live a thousand lives. I think that's why she loved this place so much."

"I think I'd like your mom," he said. "I've always felt that bookstores and libraries are places of peace. Unless you can't find what you are looking for," he added. "Then it becomes a place of frustration."

I chuckled. "What are you looking for?"

"*Paradiso* by Dante Alighieri?"

"I have a personal copy of that, but I don't have any copies for sale, unfortunately. I can order it for you if you'd like."

"Are yours in Italian or English?"

"I have both," I stated, confused.

"So, can you speak and read in Italian?"

"No, my dad did though. He was a lawyer in the city, but he had a friend originally from Sicily who would come by frequently, or call him. They only spoke in Italian to one another unless they were also talking to my mom or me. I used to sit outside the door to my dad's office and listen to them talk." I shook my head with a smile. "Didn't understand a word of it, but I loved the way it sounded. His copy is the version in Italian, my version is in English."

"So, what made you decide to get your tattoo in Italian instead of English?"

"I chose Italian as a small tribute to my dad—he loved the language, and I loved him," I said, surprised at how nice it felt to not have to censor myself for a change.

His eyes said he wanted to ask more about it, but he didn't. Instead, he stood upright.

"So, it's out of the question if I could borrow a version?"

I looked into his slate gray eyes, trying to read him. Was he trustworthy? The Italian versions of Dante's works that belonged to my dad were one of the things I cherished most in the world. So, whether I chose to lend him one or not, it would be the English one. I chewed on my lower lip in debate.

"If it will make you feel better," he took a business card off my register, grabbing a pen. "Here is my address and phone number, along with my first and last name. I will bring it back in a week, if you would like."

He slid the card across the register. I turned it over, examining it. I picked up the store phone and dialed the number he gave me.

"You don't trust me?" he laughed.

"Another thing my mom used to say is that trust is earned, not given...and I just met you yesterday."

The phone in his hand began vibrating. He flipped the screen toward me.

"See, it's a real number to my actual phone."

"You will bring it back in one week. Promise?" I asked, hanging up.

He nodded, "I'll start reading it tonight."

"Okay, I'll be right back."

I grabbed one of the books off my desk in the back and brought it to the front. He smiled as I handed it to him.

"You know...if you want to check my address, I can take you to my house." He winked.

"You better watch that," I told him.

"Watch what?" he asked with a grin, knowing full well what I was talking about.

"The flirting. The *you're in good shape* and the winking and the offering to bring me home stuff."

"Oh. That. Okay," he said, though he was still grinning. "You don't like it; I'll try to stop."

"Well, I don't think my boyfriend would like it very much."

"Ah. I see." He paused. "So?"

"So." I laughed, trying to keep it light. "A number will do. Just don't make me hunt you down."

"I won't. I'll see you around." He laughed nervously.

After he left, I brought out books from the back room, calling Austin to let him know I was restocking and then coming home. He didn't seem pleased. In fact, before I got off the phone, he told me he would see me in thirty. I knew being later than that would only set him off, so I rapidly worked for twenty minutes, and then headed home. I walked in right on time. The silence throughout the house was eerie. Then I heard Austin laughing out back. When I walked outside, he was on his phone. He held up his finger as if to say "one minute", and then he actually smiled at me. I smelled something cooking, and noticed he was holding tongs in his hand. When he got off the phone, he gave me a hug.

"Dinner will be done in about ten minutes."

"Oh, okay," I said, semi-confused. "So, that's why you wanted me home?"

"Yeah, I thought after dinner we could go on a walk or watch a movie or something."

I was thrown off, but there was no chance I was going to intentionally ask about his mood. That would spin things the opposite way. He wanted to spend time with me, like we had when we first started dating. It reminded me of before, when I was happy.

"That sounds nice, I'm going to go shower," I replied, smiling.

I showered as fast as possible, trying to soak in all the nice-Austin I could. After dinner, we decided to go on a walk. He put his arm around my shoulders as we walked down to the square. When we passed the store, he peeked inside.

"It looks good, babe." He smiled with his eyes. "I'm off in a couple days, maybe I'll come hang out with you for a few hours."

"Yeah? That would be nice. Thanks."

"Want to stop by the bar?" he asked, kissing my cheek.

"Sure, but not for long or they might put me to work," I joked.

The bar was pretty busy, with a few out-of-towners. Austin and I sat at the end of the bar with our backs to the door. We were talking when I saw Damon and Giovanni take seats across from us. Panic began to grow inside of me as I worried what Austin would do if they said anything to me. Surely, he would overreact. I began to prepare myself, just in case the night took a turn for the worse.

Austin leaned into my ear. "You want to go to the city one day this week, like for dinner or something?"

"For real? Yeah, that would be the best."

I had never been to the city before as an adult. In fact, I'd only been to the city a handful of times when I was much younger. Thoughts of how great it would be compared to this small town filled my head. Austin worked in the city, so he got to experience it every day. Madison came over a few minutes later as a rush of customers came in.

"I'm sorry to ask, but can you jump in? Please, just until this rush is over?"

My immediate reaction was to look at Austin for his permission. He shrugged his shoulders, giving me a smile.

"As long as I get free beer while she works," he said, winking at me.

"Deal," she agreed.

I jumped down from the bar stool and threw on an apron, effortlessly shifting into waitress mode. I slid Austin a beer as his was running low. I walked over to the other side of the bar, asking everybody if they were good on refills as I attempted to fill the walk-up orders coming from the tables. When I got to Damon and Giovanni, they greeted me, ordering refills.

"Noelle, can I ask you a question?" Damon asked, as I slid him his drink.

"Sure," I responded, completely aware Austin's eyes were locked on me.

"Wasn't he here last night?" he pointed to Austin across the bar.

"Yeah," I replied, "why?"

"No reason, just wondering."

I got caught up helping other customers, making my way back across the bar to where Austin was sitting. When I refilled his beer, he motioned for me to come to the other side of the bar. He pulled me toward him by the back of my neck, squeezing it enough to cause an uncomfortable pressure.

"Who the fuck are they?" he said into my ear.

"Customers, what do you mean?"

"Don't bullshit me, Noelle. One of them has been watching you ever since he got here."

"I'm serious, Austin, all they did was ask about you," I attempted to deflect his attention.

It worked; he stopped squeezing the back of my neck. "What did they ask?"

"If you were here yesterday, that's it."

"What did you say?"

"I said yes, what else would I say?"

"You should have told them to mind their own damn business, that's what," he mumbled. Then he kissed me, too rough. "I'm sorry, I just don't like him staring at you like that."

I hugged him, kissing his cheek before going back behind the bar. From that moment on, I kept my distance from Damon and Giovanni. I knew Austin would be analyzing my every move. Once Madison was back on track and the bar seemed to slow down, Austin was tipsy and ready to go. I thought Damon and Giovanni had left, but as we walked outside, they were there, leaning against the building. I heard them speaking in Italian. I discreetly smiled good night at them but when Damon returned the gesture, Austin flipped his lid.

"Why the fuck are you smiling at her like that?" he snapped.

In a flash, Austin was standing only a foot away from Damon who continued to lean back against the building. Damon was slightly taller than Austin, but a lot more muscular. Before Damon could say anything, I moved in between them.

"Austin, he was just being polite. Come on, let's go."

"Do it again, see what happens," he threatened over me. "Stay away from her."

Damon laughed, finally standing upright. "I'm sorry, am I supposed to be scared or something?"

I turned. "Thanks, Damon, that is going to really help the situation."

My eyes widened and blood drained from my face as I realized what I had just done. I felt like I was going to throw up, slowly turning back to face Austin. He looked at me with more rage than I had seen in a while.

"You're on a first name basis with this guy?" His stare burned holes in my skin.

I froze under the weight of his eyes, trying to think of anything to say.

Damon took a step forward then, and spoke in my place, telling Austin, "Hey, take it easy, man. She just—"

"She just what? Huh? I dare you to finish that sentence," Austin taunted, getting in Damon's face, before turning toward me again. "You take your ass home, now."

I opened my mouth to try to explain, but I knew better than to protest. I started the walk home alone and fast, not looking back at either of them.

At home I paced back and forth, waiting for him. He was only minutes behind me, but each second was agony. Whatever conversation happened between them after I left surely only made things worse. It was going to be horrible. I understood that when Austin arrived, the beating was going to be a bad one. My predictions came true as he charged through the front door. He yanked me up by my shirt, punching my stomach. I covered my head as he threw me into the wall. My knees buckled on impact, and I fell to the floor.

"I'm sorry, Austin," I cried. "Please, I'm sorry."

"You will be sorry, you pathetic waste of space!" he yelled.

He kicked me in the side, the steel toes of his boots digging into my ribcage. I managed to turn my body away from him. I thought it would make him stop, but he continued to kick me in the back. At that point, I knew he would keep going as long as I lay there. I rolled myself back onto my knees, attempting to crawl away from him. He stopped kicking me long enough to grab a handful of my hair. He yanked me to my feet, turning me to face him. His hands clenched my arms so tightly I thought they were going to snap in half. He said nothing as he slammed my body into the wall. My head hit the wall so hard, my ears rung. My vision went blurry as I tried not to focus on the pain throbbing on the back of my head. That was the last thing I remembered.

Chapter **Three**

I CAME TO IN THE EXACT SPOT I HAD FALLEN THE night before. As I started to get up, my body screamed to cease all movement. Pain came from all sides. I laid there for a moment, listening carefully just in case Austin was still home. I took a deep breath, holding it in as I got to my feet. In the bathroom, I slowly pulled off my shirt. My entire lower rib cage was purple. There was no telling what my back looked like, but I assumed it was just as bad. I sat down on the edge of the tub and began to cry. Why did he do this to me? I felt like I was drowning in my misery. After crying for fifteen minutes, my sadness transformed into rage. My body started to block out the pain as the anger grew inside me. I put on my running clothes, bolting out of the house at a full sprint.

I took the longest trail up to the top of the clearing, pushing myself more than I ever had as I jumped over fallen trees in the trail path. My anger was fueled by the pain I felt with each step.

Also reminding me how pathetic I was that I allowed myself to be in the situation I was in. How I was once so strong and feisty? What happened? Why hadn't I seen what was happening to me sooner? I loved Austin; maybe that was why I was so blind to what was happening to our relationship.

The word repeated in my mind: loved.

Past tense, as in, *I didn't anymore?* Or did I? I was still in love with the kind, sweet version of him who wanted to spend time with me. The version that reciprocated the feeling and made me feel cared for. That version of him was more like a rare gem now, so what was stopping me from trying to make a quick break and escape to the store that day? I knew Austin would be gone until late and yet the thought of moving everything I had in the house all at once made my stomach twist. Why? I couldn't understand.

When I got up to the top of the trail, sweat dripped from my forehead.

"Why!" I screamed into the open. "What did I do to deserve this?"

I waited, like I was going to get a response. When nothing happened, I turned my focus on my breathing, attempting to slowly calm my heart rate and emotions. I wasn't up there ten minutes before Damon and Giovanni came running in from the covered trail. They paused when they saw me.

I heard the faint sound of police radios behind them. "Where did you jump the fence?" I asked quickly.

"By the bench, next to that giant tree in the grassy area," Giovanni explained.

"Did you not notice the camera attached to the tree?"

"I guess we're busted then, because, no, we didn't," Damon admitted.

I took a few steps backward, "Correction, *you* are busted."

I ran, jumping out into a free fall. I splashed down into the lake below. I heard two more thunks as I swam to the surface. I pressed myself against the edge of the waterfall, so the police wouldn't see me. Part of the rock wall stuck out, acting as a perfect obstruction to their view. When Damon and Giovanni surfaced, they looked around. I motioned for them to come toward me. Damon was full of questions.

"They won't see—"

"Shhhhh," I looked at him.

"But, is this how—"

I put my hand over his mouth, leaning in extremely close so I didn't have to speak loudly. "I will answer your questions when they are gone."

He nodded as I removed my hand. We were only there about five minutes before I didn't hear anything.

"Don't move," I advised, pushing off the rocks to see if they were still there.

Sure enough, Max was standing at the top of the clearing.

"Noelle?" he laughed. "You know you can't be out here; I should take you in."

"Come and get me," I joked.

"Very tempting, did you see two men come this way? We caught them on the camera coming in from the short trail."

"Yeah, they're down here," I confessed.

I saw Damon and Giovanni give me a look of disbelief.

"I'm going to have to take them in," Max called down.

"Or, you could pretend you couldn't find them," I smiled.

"What am I going to get out of it?"

"Come by the store later, we can figure something out."

He laughed, "You're lucky I like you, Noelle Taylor."

"Thanks, Max."

He disappeared, walking back toward the trees. I looked at the guys.

"You guys are good."

They swam out to me. "You gave us up," Damon complained.

"Trust me, if it was anybody else, I wouldn't have. Max is different," I explained.

"How? A cop is a cop."

"Unless it's Max. We go way back."

"So, he is your friend?"

"He is my only friend. My boyfriend doesn't really like—how do I explain this— he makes it hard for me to have friends, especially *guy* friends. You saw how he acted yesterday. Max doesn't give a crap, so he hangs out with me anyway," I admitted.

"Sorry about yesterday," Damon apologized. "I didn't mean to make any trouble for you."

"It's okay. Jealousy is kind of his middle name," I attempted to joke. "Don't worry about it, really."

I swam toward the shore, climbing the trail back to the top.

"Is this how you haven't been caught?" Giovanni asked.

"Yep, they can't see you from up top if you are against the wall.

Also, I don't take the trail you came in on. They monitor that one by camera, as you can see."

"Where are you going from here?" Damon asked.

"You know, you are going to fit right in here," I stated.

"Why?"

"Because you are just as nosy as everyone else," I laughed.

Damon's cheeks flushed bright pink, which made Giovanni crack up.

"To answer your question, I'm going to dry off, get coffee, then open the book store. Do you two always run at this time or are you stalking me each morning?" I teased.

"For me, I run in the morning," Giovanni smiled. "What about you Damon?"

"Uh, yeah, I also like to run first thing in the morning."

"Well, that sounded convincing." I rolled my eyes with a smile.

The climb was steep. I started to feel my injuries as the adrenaline from jumping into the water wore off. I stopped, taking a deep breath, stretching, in an attempt to lessen the pain.

"Are you okay?" Giovanni asked.

"Yeah, I just—" How could I explain the bruises? I tried to think of something. "I fell into one of the bookcases at the store. It's hard to breathe, the bruise hurts so much. Is that normal?"

"Depends where it is and how big it is."

I began walking again, knowing the bruise was huge along my lower ribs. I made it almost to the top when I tripped over a loose rock. I fell sideways, bracing for impact of the five-foot drop off the walkway. Instead, I felt a firm arm around my ribs. I let out a short yelp as I opened my eyes to see Damon holding me up. He looked at me, confused for a moment.

"Can I see your bruise?"

I lifted up my shirt enough to reveal the bruise around my front. He reached his hand out to touch it, pausing before he made contact.

"Are you sure you didn't break a rib or something?"

I shrugged my shoulders. "I didn't go to the doctor so I don't know. Why?"

He pressed on the side of the bruise.

"Oww!" I shoved him backward toward Giovanni. "That hurts, jerk."

"I'm sorry, I'm just trying to see if anything is broken."

I held my breath while I let him check the other side. I slid my wet shirt back into place, the coolness welcome against my now throbbing bruise.

"It doesn't feel like anything is broken, but if it gets worse, I'd go to the doctor," he advised.

"Great," I muttered under my breath.

When we finally got to the clearing, Damon asked, "Do you mind if I grab a coffee with you?"

"I'm heading back," Giovanni said. "See you, Noelle."

He started the run back home. I weighed my options —Austin was in the city working, it would only be a few minutes, tops, but Austin would get angry if he found out.

"Noelle?" he said softly, interrupting my train of thought. "If you don't want me to come, that's fine."

"No, it's not that," I admitted. "Like I said, Austin doesn't really want me to have guy friends."

"What if I don't care what he wants?" he asked. "And what do *you* want?"

"I don't mind if you come, but—"

"Okay, then let's go." He started walking to the coffee shop, pausing to turn to me. "You coming?"

I walked toward him. What was I doing? This was a bad idea, but why was my body walking anyway? My brain said *tell him no thanks, go on your own.* But my feet kept on walking right beside him all the way to the coffee shop. As I greeted Alex, she got my coffee ready.

"Let me guess," she said, pointing at my damp clothes. "You either almost got caught at the clearing, or Max was the one who caught you He's always had a sweet spot for her," she tells Damon.

I laughed, taking my coffee. "Hey, he's my best friend, so the feeling is mutual."

She turned to take Damon's order, looking back and forth at both of us. She started laughing. "And you got caught up in the middle of it today?"

"He's not going to deny or admit to anything," I interrupted.

She shook her head as she made his order. We walked out, heading back toward the bar.

"Noelle, I'm really sorry for yesterday. I hope I didn't cause any problems," he apologized again.

"It's okay. That's just how he is, ever since I moved in with him."

"How long have you been together?"

"Two and a half years."

"And he still acts like that?" he said in disbelief. "I mean, he acted all territorial last night. I thought you two just started dating or something."

"I think he had it out for you when you came in. He said he didn't like the way you were looking at me."

He almost spit out his coffee. "What?"

"I'm sure it was nothing, he likes to make something out of nothing all the time."

"No, it wasn't nothing." He stole a glance at me before looking down at his coffee. "I'll admit, I really couldn't take my eyes off you last night."

"What?" I blushed, but immediately felt the pit in my stomach expanding. "Damon, you shouldn't say things like that."

He laughed, "Did you want me to lie? Oh no, I wasn't checking you out or anything." He played it off. His tone made me chuckle as we stopped at the corner. "He was just seeing things."

"I have to go get ready to open the store."

"I'll see you later then."

The more I moved the worse my body ached. My shower was more like a rinse and putting on clothes was a challenge. I decided to let my hair air dry as there was no chance I was going to be able to move and twist my upper body like I normally did. I packed up some of my books. If Austin noticed they were gone, it would be easy to explain that I'd brought them to the store to read as I worked.

I opened the store, having to restock multiple times throughout the day due to the increasing number of book sales. I never realized how many people passed through our town, stopping to explore the *little shops*, as they like to put it.

Damon came in around lunch to return *Paradiso*. He sat it on the front counter.

"You read that in one night?" I asked in disbelief.

"No, I had read most of it before I moved. I'm still unpacking my home library and office. I couldn't find it in any of the boxes, so I assumed it got lost in the move. I finally found it today."

"When did you move here?"

"Almost two weeks ago now, we moved from the suburbs outside the city."

My eyebrows raised. "And you moved here, to this tiny town? Why?"

"Because my family moved. My brother and his wife bought the house next door to me and my parents bought the house across the street."

"Okay...but why?"

"My dad was the one who wanted to move here," he laughed. "We just followed. He claims it's because he likes the small-town life as opposed to the city. My brother and I think he's going to retire from the business soon and that's the real reason. He hasn't said much other than that, though."

I pursed my lips, giving it some thought. "I guess it's a nice place to retire to. I don't know, growing up here I have a very different perspective."

"Which is what?"

"It's too small—you tell one person something and within

a week everyone knows a new version of the truth you told. I'd love to go someplace where no one knows me."

"I feel that same way about the city."

My brows furrowed in confusion. "People talk about you? Are you famous?"

He laughed. "No, but my family is well-known so it feels like many people know me. The same situation happens in the city, it's just with smaller amounts of people in comparison to here."

"I've never thought about it like that before. That's an interesting viewpoint."

Damon was still there as Max came in. I set down the books I was restocking and gave him a hug. He looked to Damon, holding out his hand.

"Max Reeves, and you are one of the guys from the camera view this morning," he laughed.

"Damon Amoretti," Damon said, shaking his hand. "Yeah, that was me."

"Amoretti—as in *the Amoretti* family?" he asked.

"That's the one."

Max began speaking to him in Italian. Damon looked surprised but responded in Italian as well.

"Hey," I interrupted, "English only or outside you go."

To my surprise, they left. I was baffled by their actions. Whatever conversation they were having must have been important. They came back inside, laughing. Max said something to me, which I ignored for a second before turning to him.

"Oh, you're talking to me now?" I said sarcastically.

"Sorry, it was important," he explained.

I smiled, letting out a short laugh. "You're lucky I like you, Max Reeves." I finished putting the books up before I turned to him. "Want to go to the bar tonight?"

"Hell yeah, what time?"

"I'll have to make Austin dinner first, so how about eight. I'll meet you there?"

He made a throw-up noise as I mentioned Austin. "Tell me one more time why you are with him again? He's such a dick."

I couldn't help but snort. "You never liked him, so your opinion doesn't count."

"Yeah, yeah. Is he going to let you come or should I pick you up?"

I thought about it for a moment—Austin's moods were hit and miss.

"Actually, you might want to pick me up."

"All right, see you at eight."

He hugged me once before leaving. Damon looked at me, tilting his head to the side a bit. His smile slowly grew across his lips.

"Can I ask a question?"

I turned to him, "I won't guarantee an answer, but you can ask."

"You said Austin doesn't like you to have friends. But you hang out with Max. Why is he different?"

"Well," I sighed. "First of all, Max doesn't give a crap about what Austin says. Secondly, Max has been my best friend since I was a kid. Thirdly, Austin is slightly afraid of him."

"Why?"

I bit my lip debating on opening up or not. What could it hurt? It happened so long ago.

"A couple months after I started dating Austin, we got into a fight and Max was there. Austin called me some not-so-nice things and I guess he sort of grabbed me by the throat. Max stepped in and practically beat the life out of him. Ever since then, when Max shows up or wants to hang out, Austin doesn't say a word."

I began to wonder what Max would do if I told him about all the other times Austin had hurt me. I was also moving out into the apartment so what would it matter to speak about it now? Max would probably think a lot of the same things I had been thinking; I'm sure he'd also wonder what happened to the old me?

Damon nodded, thinking for a moment. "So, in order for me to get on the list of Noelle's friends, all I have to do is beat the shit out of him?" he asked.

I chuckled. "Please don't do that, I'm sure he will come around."

Even though I knew Austin would never come around, I was hoping it would convince Damon to stay clear of him.

Chapter **Four**

I WAS GETTING AUSTIN'S DINNER PLATE READY AS HE walked through the door. *Here we go,* I thought as he came into the kitchen.

Kissing me on the cheek, Austin grabbed his plate. I joined him at the kitchen table.

"How was your day?" I asked.

"It was good, I'm tired though. I don't know why, but I'm exhausted."

I looked at him, thinking about how he would react to me going out with Max that night. I decided to wait until dinner was over. We finished eating and I did the dishes. Austin was watching television when I came into the living room. I rubbed his shoulders from behind, kissing his cheek.

"Is it okay if I go to the bar with Max for a little bit?"

I held my breath, waiting for a reaction. He tilted his head back on the couch cushions to look up at me.

"Sure, be home by ten."

"But that's only two hours," I pointed out, as gently as possible. "How about midnight?"

"I'll think about it."

I got a text from Max: *slight change of plans, bring a bathing suit.* I wondered if we were going to the clearing again. We used to hang out there all the time before Austin came around. I went upstairs, throwing my bathing suit into my purse when I heard the doorbell ring. Austin had answered it already as I came down the stairs. I turned to him, kissing him once.

"See you at midnight," he said, smiling like he was the most perfect, understanding boyfriend in the world. I kissed him again, happy he was letting me stay out later than he said. I shut the front door behind me, smiling at Max. As we started walking toward the center of town, I caught his eye.

"So, what's the new plan?"

"Bar first, then we're going swimming."

I could tell by the way he smiled we were going exactly where I had hoped. On the way, I saw Damon and Giovanni strolling through the streets. I wondered what they were up to. We sat at the bar for a bit, having a few drinks as we caught up on each other's lives. It was more like me catching up on his life, as I didn't have much of a life outside of Austin. I did tell him about the process of opening the store and how it was doing. I teased him about not having a girl-friend like I always did, before trying to convince him to go on a date with Alex. I changed into my bathing suit at the bar before we left. Max pulled out a bottle of Fireball as we hit the top of the clearing.

I laughed, "You bought that?"

"Hell, yeah."

His smile was exhilarating. It reminded me of all the times we snuck out to the clearing together as reckless teenagers. We were fearless and up for anything. It was a feeling I wanted to cling to. We climbed down to the bottom of the small cliff, making our way to the spot we always went to. Max disappeared into the edge of the woods, reappearing with some fallen branches to start a fire. As he got the fire going, I sat on the ground, looking at the dark scenery. At night, it was kind of spooky. It gave me chills which made me feel a bit more excited. Max sat beside me, taking a drink of Fireball before handing it to me.

"I have to tell you something," he said quietly, looking out into the water.

"What?" I reached up, touching his shoulder.

"A couple weeks ago, I applied for a temporary job in the city as an undercover agent," he paused, turning to me. "I find out tomorrow if I got the job or not."

My heart plummeted into my stomach as I tried to swallow the lump in my throat. Max was my rock, the person who I could call as an escape from Austin, anytime, without question. I wanted him to stay, selfishly keeping him in town as my safety blanket. The thing was, Max always had a reason for doing something. He was thoughtful and genuine in each decision he made. I knew it couldn't have been easy for him to apply for this job no matter how temporary. The least I could do was be the supportive friend, but I wasn't quite sure what to say.

"I'm sure you got it, Max, you're good at your job," I replied. "Except I heard that you can't nab this one suspect. She comes to the clearing and you catch her all the time, but she always manages to escape." I smiled, trying to lighten the mood.

My stupid humor worked: He laughed. "Yeah, there's something about her, I just can't bring her in. Not sure why."

"Either way, you'll be great at what you do." I pulled him into a hug. "I hope you get it."

He shook his head. "That's what I'm worried about."

I leaned back, looking at him, confused.

"When I said temporary, I meant I don't know for how long. It could be a month. Could be four years, I just don't know. During that time, I can't have any contact with the ones I care about, just in case I get caught as an undercover agent. That means—"

"You won't be able to talk to me," I interrupted, sadly. I stood up, pulling him to his feet. "Max, either way, it's temporary, and you are going to come back. Isn't it when you bust the guys, or whatever your assignment is, then you come home?"

"Yeah."

"Then if you get the job, go to the city, get the job done, come back." I gave him a supportive smile. "I'll still be here."

He put his hand on my cheek, shaking his head as if that would clear his thoughts.

"Let's swim. Enough stressful talk for one night."

He pulled off his shirt, tossing it to the side. I had slid my shorts down halfway when I froze. Nearby, I heard the distinct sound of twigs crunching underfoot.

"Did you hear that?" I whispered to Max.

He nodded, moving me behind him. It made me nervous to see Max on edge, and yet a bit of adrenaline began to pump through my system. We waited for less than a minute, before two dark figures came through the trees. I held my breath. When the fire lit up their faces, I exhaled. It was Damon and Giovanni.

"What are you guys doing here?" I wondered, relieved.

"Exploring," Giovanni laughed. "Although we got a bit lost. Then we saw the fire and used that to lead us out."

"What are *you* doing here?" Damon asked, pointedly, looking from a shirtless Max and me with no pants on.

"Swimming."

"Feel free to join us," Max offered turning toward me, "Come on."

I moved to walk behind him.

"I don't have swim trunks on," he stated.

I laughed, "Damon, you jumped into the water this morning in your workout clothes, which is basically what you have on now. But, suit yourself."

I pulled my shirt over my head, tossing it next to the fire. He said something in Italian to which both Giovanni and Max started laughing.

"Oh, shit, I forgot you speak Italian," he said to Max, covering his face.

"What did he say?" I asked.

"He'll tell you later," Max smiled. "I'm almost sure of it."

I crossed my arms. "No, tell me now."

Max picked me up, "Okay, he said let him know if it's cold."

"If what's cold?"

With that he tossed me over the edge. I splashed down, feeling the cool water on my skin. I broke the surface only to see Max jump in beside me.

"Not funny and not fair," I shouted, laughing as I splashed him. "That's not what he said."

I looked to Damon. He took his shoes and socks off and dove in next to us. When he surfaced, I looked around us then back up to the cliff. "Where's Giovanni?" I asked.

"He's gone home to Grace."

"Who's Grace?"

"His wife."

How old is he? I thought to myself.

"Why do you look surprised?" he asked.

"He looks so young to be married already," I admitted.

Damon shrugged. "He found his *one,* and married her."

"Which makes it sound so easy," I said, laughing.

Max said something to Damon in Italian. I let out a groan before pushing myself into the center of the lake where the water was its deepest.

"Seriously, this is supposed to be fun, guys. Not annoying."

Next thing I knew it was quiet. There was nothing but the crackling of the fire. I looked around to see only water around me. They were under the water–they had to be.

"This isn't funny, Max," I said, waiting to hear him giggle.

They popped out of the water in front of me. I screamed, splashing them away. We swam around until the muscles in my arms and legs were too tired to go on, then finally got out and lay in the grass next to the fire. Max and Damon were on either side of me.

"So, why were you and Giovanni running through the streets earlier?" I asked, my thoughts returning to earlier that evening.

He shrugged. "It's good to know the area where you live in the daylight and at nightfall. We've been walking around and running the streets for a few days now to get better accustomed to the street names and layout of the town."

"I could've just drawn you a map."

He chuckled. I closed my eyes, then felt a light on my face.

"What the hell is that from, Noelle?"

I opened my eyes to see Max sitting up straight next to me, his phone flashlight shining over my abdomen.

His tone was accusatory, and I knew exactly who he was going to blame it on. He was right, but I couldn't let him know. It was my fault he hit me anyway, I ruined a perfectly good night. He was trying to change; I knew that much.

"Relax, it's from the bookstore. I fell yesterday trying to restock books. How did you just now notice it?"

"I'm sorry, next time I'll be sure to check you out *before* we get into the water."

"Fine, you do that." I laughed, wanting to brush it off.

"Did you notice it?" Max asked Damon.

"Yeah," he said uncertainly. "I saw it after we got out of the water this morning."

I sat up, taking a sharp swig of the whisky we brought. Moving closer to the fire, I tried to soak up the warmth.

"Are you cold?" Max asked.

I nodded and Max threw my shorts to me. I slid them on, holding my hands out for my shirt.

"Where is your shirt?" he asked.

I pointed to where it should have been, but it wasn't there. I squinted at Max.

"Not funny, give me my shirt."

"Noelle, I don't have it, I promise."

I walked around, looking everywhere for my shirt. I talked myself through where I had thrown it. Looking toward the fire, I saw the corner of it.

"Oh, no." I walked over, picking up what was left of it. "I threw it into the fire on accident. Now what am I going to do? I can't go home without a shirt."

I sat down in between them, freezing. Damon handed me his.

"Here, you can have mine."

I took it, sliding it on. "Thanks. I don't know how I'm going to explain this to Austin. I feel like coming home in another guy's shirt is worse than coming home with just my bathing suit top on."

"I'll take care of it," Max assured me.

Damon's shirt was warm and smelled like him. I had to resist the urge to bring a handful of the soft fabric to my nose to breathe it in. We sat there drinking and talking until it was time to go. Damon put out the fire as we gathered up our stuff.

The light from the street lamps lit up the sidewalk, splashing across Damon, his muscles perfectly defined. He had another tattoo on his chest. I couldn't tell what it was from my angle.

"I'll see you guys later." He did that guy handshake-pat on the shoulder thing with Max and then nodded in my direction before he crossed to the other sidewalk toward the gated neighborhood.

"Bye, Damon, and thanks for the shirt," I noted.

As Max and I continued to walk, he put his arm around my shoulders. I felt my body getting tense as we got closer to the house.

"You okay?" he asked. "Don't worry about anything, I'll talk to Austin and everything will be all right. If it's not, you call me. I know his mouth gets the best of him sometimes."

I laughed, knowing he was so much more than right. The silence fell between us for a moment before Max let out a sigh.

"Noelle, that bruise—you'd tell me if it wasn't really from the bookcase?"

My body tensed. "What do you mean?"

"I mean, you'd come to me if Austin crossed that line with you again, right?"

"I'm clumsy Max, you know that the best out of anyone."

He seemed to be debating. I wrapped one arm around his, leaning my head against him for a moment. The silence came upon us once more as we took in the night air. I opened the front door to be greeted by a confused Austin. I quickly diverted his attention to Max.

"Max wants to talk to you," I stated.

I turned, hugging Max goodbye. I went upstairs, jumping in

the shower. When I got out, I put pajamas on, going downstairs to look for Austin. He was shutting off the television as I walked into the room. I quickly tried to judge whether I needed to bolt or stay there. His face seemed oddly casual. I stood still, waiting for him to say something. He walked past me, grabbing my hand to lead me upstairs. He crawled into bed, motioning for me to do the same. When I did, he kissed me, pulling me closer to him.

"I love you, Noelle."

My face showed the shock. Austin had not told me he loved me in a long time. He kissed me once more before laying his head on his pillow. I leaned into him, resting my head next to his.

"I love you, too," I whispered. Maybe it was still possible to salvage what we had; as long as I didn't do anything to provoke him or mess up the situation, we would be fine. I just had to remember that. I fell asleep easily that night.

Chapter **Five**

THAT NEXT MORNING, AUSTIN WOKE ME UP BY KISSING me softly. I turned to kiss him back. He climbed on top of me, pulling his shirt off. I hugged him to me, feeling a hint of what it used to be between us. But when he pulled my shorts and underwear off, I felt rushed and anxious. I tried to sound firm with the words I was speaking to him so he took them seriously.

"Austin, stop, slow down."

He was like this each time he wanted to be intimate. It was like it couldn't happen fast, or frequently, enough. Many times, I stopped him or told him I wasn't in the mood. That morning, I just wanted him to hold me like he had the night before.

"Come on, Noelle, it's been too long. It's time."

He kissed my neck forcefully. His hands moved down my body. It no longer felt like it used to, it felt like he was thinking only about what he wanted. He didn't care how I felt; he only wanted to please himself. Just like so many times before he disregarded how I felt in this situation that should be a moment of beauty between two people. I'd given in many times before as it was easier than facing his rage when I denied him. Not this morning. No. Between hanging out with Max the night before at the clearing and the back-and-forth banter with Damon I'd been given a glimpse of the old me. The freedom to do and say what I wanted was electrifying. That feisty version of myself was still in there, hiding behind my fears of retaliation Austin would take anytime she surfaced. My heartrate began to race, my breath quickening as he lowered his weight on me. I felt his hard length pressed against me through his boxers.

"I said stop!" I screamed, my hands shaking, yet firm as I pushed against him as hard as I could.

He let out a growl, "Fuck you, Noelle!"

He got up, punching the wall on his way into the bathroom. I curled up in a ball, pulling my shorts back on. He continued to yell at me as he got ready for work.

"What is wrong with you, stupid bitch? You need to figure your shit out and get it together."

He slammed the door shut behind him. I waited a couple minutes, trying to figure out what emotion was more prominent. I was hurt because he didn't care, mad because he thought he had a right to say when it was *time*, and scared because I knew he was stronger than I was. If he wanted to, he could force me into it.

I flung myself from bed, threw on my running clothes, and sprinted through the front door—I needed out of that house. I ran as hard as I could to the clearing. By the time I got to the top, I was crying. Damon and Giovanni were standing near the edge of the trail as I broke through the woods. I stopped, trying to calm down. I turned away from them, taking off my shirt to wipe my face with it. I was hoping they would just think I was sweating. I turned toward them, shirt in hand.

"Hey!" I tried to put on a smile. "Fancy meeting you two here, coffee today?"

"Yeah." Damon waited for me to put my shirt back on. When I didn't, he laughed a little. "Are you going like that?"

"I mean, you've seen me in my bathing suit, which has less fabric than this, what's left?"

"Naked?" Damon smiled a goofy smile.

Giovanni covered his face, embarrassed by his brother. I couldn't help but laugh after the morning I had. I got really close to him, so our faces were inches apart.

"Maybe one day..." I said as softly as I could, "in your dreams."

I saw the goose bumps rise on his arms. Giggling, I turned toward Giovanni.

"Are you coming for coffee?"

"Sure, I'll tag along today. Damon says the coffee is pretty good."

With that, we started the run back to town. I threw my shirt on to cover my bruises from the customers at the store before going in. I grabbed my coffee, waiting on the guys to get theirs. We walked around the small park as we drank our coffee. When Giovanni finished his and then left to meet up with Grace, I turned to Damon.

"Can I meet her sometime...Grace?" I said, thinking it would be good to have another woman talk to around here.

"I'm sure I can arrange that."

"NOELLE!" I turned to see Max sprinting toward me in his uniform. He stopped in front of me. "I got the job."

I jumped up, hugging him. "Congratulations!"

He shook his head. "I didn't accept or decline yet. I wanted your opinion."

"I say take it," I rolled my eyes. "You are being dramatic. You know you want it, take it. You said it was temporary anyway. I'll still be here when you get back."

"He said I'd only be gone a couple months."

"Take it, Max Reeves. Call him. Right now!"

He did, turning and taking a few steps away for privacy.

"What job did he get?"

"Uh," I hesitated, "a job in the city. It's temporary but I think he's going to love it."

"I think he might. No matter how much I complain about the city it really is a beautiful place full of crazies. I'm sure he'll be more entertained there than here."

I pulled my lower lip between my teeth as it all began to sink in. Max put his arm around me, rejoining us with a wide grin.

"I'm going to miss you the entire time. Who's going to be my best friend and partner in crime now?"

He smiled. "Damon can stand in for me."

Damon almost dropped his coffee. I laughed—it wouldn't be all bad, I guess. Damon proved he was up for anything the night before.

"Are you up for that challenge?" I teased him.

"Fuck, yeah," his eyes sparkled as his lips parted in a lazy grin, "challenge accepted."

"Good." I smiled at Damon. Then I turned to Max. "When do you leave?"

"Tomorrow morning."

"Come by the bar tonight and we can celebrate during my shift." I elbowed Damon softly. "You can come, too."

I hugged Max once more before saying goodbye to both of them. They started their own conversation as I ran home to get ready to open the store. By ten o'clock I had seven texts from Austin apologizing to me about what happened that morning. I typed 'it's not okay Austin' before staring at it. My thumb hovered over the send button, the resolve I had to speak the truth to him dissipating with each second. With a heavy sigh I erased 'not' and sent the message before pocketing my phone once more. How else could I respond? I didn't want him even angrier by provoking him. I reminded him I had a shift at the bar so he would be prepared to grab dinner after work. I knew he wouldn't cook his own dinner at home.

Max showed up at the bar around seven. I had the kitchen cook him his favorite plate of heaping loaded nachos. Damon got there an hour later. I got them both situated as I helped other customers. When it was slow, I took my break to join them. Max was excited, I could tell. He didn't say much about what he would be doing. In fact, he only said it was a job in the city. He didn't even tell anyone else about the fact that it was undercover. I took that to mean that no one else was supposed to know, so I didn't say anything. My break went by so fast I didn't even realize it was over until Madison came to get me. I jumped back behind the bar, laughing and talking with the guys. I heard Max attempt to tell Damon what to do about Austin. I gave Max a look as he toned down his conversation.

On the walk home, we parted with Damon at the corner. Max turned to me as we came to my house. Standing on the front porch he hugged me. I didn't want to let him go. We stood there for a long time, even after Austin pulled into the driveway. As he walked to us, he paused.

"So, it's true, you took a job in the city?" he asked.

I wondered how Austin knew already before it dawned on me. The gossip in this town spread like wildfire. Max had not only shouted the news excitedly in the middle of the park for all to hear, but also talked about it at the bar. On top of that, I was sure his department already knew—there weren't many officers, but enough to go home and tell their spouses.

"Yeah, it's true," he stated dryly.

"Good luck," Austin snickered, giving him a dismissive nod. "I'm sure you have your work cut out for you. The city is a big place." He turned to me, saying, "I'm getting a shower, are you coming in soon?"

"Yeah, in just a few minutes."

I moved over, letting him by. Once he shut the front door, I relaxed a little bit. He seemed in a good mood. I looked up at Max.

"So, this is it, huh?" I asked. "I can't call you or anything?"

He laughed. "Unfortunately, not."

"How dangerous is it? Your assignment?"

"I don't know. I find out tomorrow."

I bit my lip. "But you'll be careful, right?"

He laughed, putting one hand on my cheek. "Yes, I will be careful. Stop worrying about me, Noelle, I'll be fine."

"I can't help it." I smiled a little, only to cover up my sadness.

He looked at his phone. "I have to go get packed."

I squeezed him tightly before letting go. As he started his walk home, I knew I needed one more hug. I called after him, running up to him, hugging him one last time. He kissed the top of my head.

"I love you, Max Reeves."

He smiled, fighting back tears of his own. "I love you, too, Noelle Taylor."

I let go, my smile weak but there. If I didn't let him go now I probably wouldn't ever. I walked back to the house, waving goodbye as he disappeared around the corner. I heard Austin getting out of the shower as I locked the front door behind me. As I got ready for bed, I could feel Austin watching me.

"What?" I asked.

"Why are you carrying your phone around with you?" he asked, annoyed.

I looked down at my phone. "I don't know, what does that matter?"

"Let me see it," he ordered.

"Why?"

He took a step toward me, raising his voice. "Let. Me. See. It," he repeated.

I handed him my phone, watching as he went through it. I felt like a child waiting for a punishment. I saw him reading my texts from Max for that day. When he was finished, he tossed my phone back at me, then walked away. I didn't know what to do with myself. I just finished getting ready for bed.

Crawling in next to him, my phone suddenly went off, which was unusual. I picked it up and saw a message from a private number. I opened it out of curiosity.

There on the screen was a picture of Austin kissing a blonde girl. The next one, she was on his lap, making out with him. I jumped out of bed in a full rage, turning on the light.

He sat up, looking at me like I was crazy.

"Who is she?" I asked through tears, showing him the pictures.

I watched as his face turned from confused to desperate. His furrowed brows raising as he examined the photos on display for him. He grabbed a handful of his own hair, giving it a tug.

"Um-she's nobody, Noelle. Who-uh-who sent you those?"

"If she's nobody then why are you kissing her?" I yelled.

He sighed. "There was alcohol involved, I'm sorry. I didn't mean it, she's nothing, Noelle, I love *you*," he put his hands on my arms.

I shoved him away, disgusted. "You're sorry you got caught, that's all."

I turned toward the door, beginning to walk downstairs. He grabbed me by the arm. When I felt how hard his grip was, I knew I was in trouble.

"It's your fault, you stupid bitch, if you didn't tell me *no* all the time, I wouldn't have to get it somewhere else."

I turned to him. "You slept with her? You know what, Austin? I'm done. We're done!"

He slapped me in the face before shoving me against the wall. My cheek stung.

"Let's get one thing straight," he spat. "You are mine. If you try to leave, I will kill you." He laughed, pressing me harder against the wall. "Besides, now that Max is leaving, no one else will want to put up with your sorry ass. Who else do you have? Get back in bed."

"I'm not sleeping with you." I attempted to stand up for myself once again, even though I knew it was no use. This resistance only awarded me a punch to my head. He grabbed me by the neck, throwing me onto the bed. He climbed on top of me, wrapping his hands around my throat. He started to squeeze.

His face was red with rage, the veins in his neck and forearms straining against his skin. The intensity of his eyes, so wide the whites of them were revealed to me, shot a new form of fear straight through my body. My shoulders tensed as I began to squirm underneath him. I reached for his arms, trying to move his hands away from my neck.

"When I tell you something, it is not a question, it's an order. You do what I say, when I say, as I say it. Understood?"

I tried to push him off of me, but my fight only made him squeeze tighter. A pricking feeling started in my face and head. He pulled me toward him, shoving me backward into the bed.

"I said, understood?"

I nodded as best I could. He leaned in closer to me.

"You know, I could just kill you now for trying to leave me. But I think you have learned your lesson, right?"

I again tried to nod. He let go, rolling over to lie back down. I started to cough, struggling to get enough air into my lungs. I didn't dare move from the bed. I quietly cried into the pillow. Was he right? Was it my fault because I wouldn't give myself to him every time he'd wanted it? My fear of him turned into self-hatred as I lay there thinking about what he said. If I'd had sex with him, he wouldn't have cheated on me. Why didn't I just give it up like he wanted? But then why would I get mad when he finds it with someone else? By the time I fell asleep, I had convinced myself it was once again my fault.

On my run the next morning, I got to the clearing early, closing my eyes to listen to all the sounds of nature. I tried to clear my mind. If I thought about anything from the night before, I was afraid I'd break down. Then I heard Damon coming through the trees, it was his normal run time already? I didn't turn around. I wasn't ready to give up the peaceful sounds I was focusing on.

"Noelle?"

"Yeah?" I responded, not moving or opening my eyes.

"You okay?"

I couldn't help but laugh. "As okay as I can be, given the circumstances."

I knew he thought I meant Max leaving, but I was thinking of those pictures, still on my phone and permanently burned into my mind. I finally turned toward him to see Giovanni standing next to him. I smiled, trying to sound more okay than I felt.

"Sorry, it's tough. I miss him already."

"He'll be back before you know it. I'm sure he'll call when he isn't busy."

"I wish. He can't have contact with anybody the entire time

he's there. Which means at least two months without talking to him."

"What exactly is he doing?" Giovanni asked.

"If he didn't tell you, I can't either. I'm sorry."

Before anyone could say anything else, a girl came running through the trail. Giovanni greeted her, putting his arm around her shoulders. I heard police radios behind her.

"What trail did you come in?" Giovanni asked her.

"The one with the bench and big tree, you said to take that one."

"No, I said *don't* take that one." He turned to me, "Sorry."

We all knew what to do, except for the girl. We took a quick jump into the water, the girl following our lead. Once we were tucked under the ledge, she turned toward me.

"I'm Grace," she said, laughing as she extended her hand to me above the water. "You are?"

"Noelle," I whispered. "Nice to meet you."

I waited patiently before hearing the radio get closer.

"They're coming down the side. They probably heard us jump," I turned to Grace. "This is going to be super awkward, but trade me shirts."

"What?"

"They have you on camera, the back of you. I need to wear the same outfit. Give me your shirt. Our shorts are close enough in color, they won't pick that up."

She did as I said. As I threw on her shirt, I started to swim-walk toward the land. Damon grabbed my hand.

"Won't they arrest you?"

I smiled, "Well, yeah, but it's better than all four of us. Besides, it's not the first time I've been caught out here."

He dropped my hand reluctantly, letting me walk into the path of the officer.

"Noelle Taylor," he stated. "Again! Did you not learn your lesson the first time I arrested you for trespassing?"

"My goal was to not get caught again, Officer Wells." I shrugged.

"Do you know criminal trespassing can land you, at minimum, thirty days in jail?"

"You can't charge me with anything criminal as I didn't commit any crime on the land to which I am trespassing. That means I get a ticket or fine to be paid within thirty days, no jail time," I explained.

He shook his head, and grinned. "You really are your father's daughter."

He walked me down the trail to his patrol car, giving me a towel he had in his trunk before getting in. He then drove us the three blocks to the police station.

"I think your ticket should be $250," he suggested. "What do you think?"

"I think I should get another warning."

"Your reasoning, Ms. Taylor?"

"It's my second offense, yes. However, I did not resist arrest or commit a crime. Furthermore, a fine of that nature would best suit a case of trespassing on private property with little to no damage to said property."

"Tell me, when are you taking the bar exam?"

"I'm not." I thought of my father. Fear of letting him down is something I've battled with since he passed. "I can't."

"He would've been so proud of you, Noelle," he said. "Don't think the results of one test would ever disappoint him—nothing you could do would ever disappoint him."

I nodded, feeling tears coming on.

"Listen...just don't get caught again." He winked at me. "Go on."

"Thank you, Officer Wells."

I ran down to the coffee shop, and asked Alex for my usual. As I was walking back home to get cleaned up, I saw Damon, Giovanni, and Grace walking toward me. I stopped, waiting for them to catch up.

"I thought you would have already gotten coffee," I said.

"How are you out already?" Giovanni said in disbelief.

"My dad was a lawyer," I explained. "They had nothing to charge me with, they could only give me a fine."

"How much was it?" Giovanni asked. "We'll help pay it."

"Like I said, my dad was a lawyer, I didn't get a fine either." I shifted my weight to my toes and back giving them a wink.

"Seriously?" Giovanni said in disbelief. "Remind me to hire you if I ever need it."

"Well, I'm not a lawyer, I just know the law. My dad quizzed me when I was younger and I helped him prep for cases. I wanted to go to law school, but—" I stopped, running my fingers through my wet ponytail, "then things...happened."

"What do you mean?" Damon asked.

Yep, I should have seen that coming. I took a sip of my coffee, gathering my thoughts and checking my emotions. No matter how long ago it was, they were my parents, the two people I loved more than anything.

"My parents—they were killed three years ago." Damon's shoulders slumped, his gaze falling to the sidewalk we were standing on. When his eyes flickered back to mine, they were apologetic, his expression pained.

"What happened?" Grace asked.

"Grace, hon, that's not—"

"No, it's okay," I reassured him. "My dad took on the head of some big organization in the city that was threatening another company. I helped him prep for weeks beforehand. That final day, he took my mom with him so she could be there when they announced the verdict. He normally wouldn't take us with him, for our own safety. He won his case and the guy was put away for life. But that night, after they went out to celebrate, someone gunned them down. The police said it was probably revenge." I paused. "So, I won't take the bar exam."

Grace didn't say anything else, just hugged me. I smiled at the kind gesture.

"I have to go get ready to open the store," I told her. "If you are free, come by later."

She nodded, "I'll see you later then."

Chapter **Six**

BUSINESS AT THE STORE WAS SLOW ALL DAY. I BROUGHT up the pictures of Austin and the blonde again, staring at them, trying to understand what was going on in his mind. I was on the verge of breaking down just as Grace came through the door. I quickly put the phone away.

"Hey, Noelle," she greeted me.

I looked around the store to make sure no one was shopping.

"Hey, do you want to grab a coffee with me?"

"I'm down for anything," she said, her warm smile brightening her face.

I locked up the store, walking with her across the street. We claimed a back table in the corner as our own.

"How long have you and Giovanni been married?"

"Just about three years, although our story has an interesting start," she smiled cheekily.

"What do you mean?"

"Well, I went to a club in the city with my friends. The funny thing is, I didn't want to go out that night, so I was being a sourpuss and sulking at the bar. What made it worse was that the guys there kept asking me to dance. I just wanted to be left alone so of course I was wearing my attitude. Giovanni approached me and said, 'you look upset', to which I replied, 'and you look desperate' before walking out." She scoffed, shaking her head at the memory. "I made it to the corner of the street before he came running after me. He offered to give me a ride home. When I shot him down again, he asked if I was hungry."

"If you were hungry?" I laughed. "Why would he ask that?"

"That's what I asked him. He said it was because when he's hungry he gets irritated so he thought that's why I was giving him an attitude." She smiled to herself thinking back. "It was so…innocent, that I had to laugh."

"What did he say?"

"Nothing. He just held out his arm with a smile. I debated whether to go, but there was something in his eyes that made me join him. We went to a little pizza place down the street and talked for almost two hours."

"So, is that when you knew he was the one?"

"No. He walked me home after that. When he asked if he could see me again, I told him 'If he was lucky' and then went inside." She paused, turning her wedding ring on her finger. "It was a couple days later that he showed up outside my apartment with flowers asking me to dinner. After that, we started to hang out more and more."

"So, there's no mysterious sign to knowing the one?"

She shook her head. "No, not really. But Giovanni made me laugh. I think I figured he was my one when I concluded that I'd do anything for him, just as I felt he would do anything for me. Love feels like..." she stopped mid-sentence, thinking. "Honestly, it feels like complete trust and warmth. Even when he's having the worst possible day, he still asks me how mine went. And I always try to make him feel better. It's euphoric in every way. There's no specific sign, but you just know it when you feel it."

Just then, Damon came in, smiling at me.

"Go away, this is girl talk," Grace joked.

He put his hands up. "I just came to check on Noelle after this morning. I know Max just left, but I want to make sure I'm doing my stand-in partner in crime duties." He sat down next to Grace across from me. "So how are you holding up?"

"I'm falling apart," I admitted.

The bell to the front door rang. My stomach twisted as I looked up to see Austin. My heart sank. I was in big trouble with Damon being there. When Austin saw him, he walked closer to me.

"What is he doing here?"

"Austin, it's a coffee shop, anybody can come here."

He turned toward Damon, who was now standing next to Grace.

"Did I not tell you to stay away from her?" Austin said fiercely.

Damon didn't give him any attention. I was guessing this was for my sake. Grace came over to me, hugging me.

"Text me for anything," she whispered into my ear.

I nodded and before I knew what was happening Austin

grabbed Grace's wrist, yanking her away from me. In the blink of an eye, Damon had Austin's arm twisted behind his back. The entire coffee shop was silently watching everything unfold.

"Touch her again—*either* of them—and I break your arm," he threatened. "Understand?" When he let go, he turned to me. "See you around."

With that, they left. Austin dragged me out by my arm. He tore open the passenger's side door, throwing me into the front seat. I was already apologizing as we turned down our road. He lit a cigarette. He knew I loathed when he smoked, that's why he did it, I guessed. It wasn't going to be good when we got home, and I could no longer call Max to get away from him. When we got home, he snatched me by the elbow.

"Did you think you wouldn't get caught with him?" he snapped, taking one last sharp inhale on his cigarette. He held it between two fingers, like he was showing it to me for some reason, bringing it closer and closer to my face. *He wouldn't.* I could feel the fiery tip burning so nearly touching my cheek. And then, in one swift motion, he put his cigarette out on my arm. I screamed as it seared my skin. He covered my mouth, pulling me closer to him by my neck.

"Scream again and I'll give you something to really scream about." He tossed me up the porch steps like I was nothing more than a ragdoll. "Go make dinner, you useless piece of shit."

I ran into the house crying. I did as he said, making his plate as he sat down at the table. When I sat down next to him, he laughed at me. He took my plate from me, handing me a piece of bread.

"You can eat this, then go to bed."

"But—" I didn't even see it coming—he backhanded me across the face. My cheek stung as he ripped the bread in half.

"Now you get half. You could lose a few pounds anyway. You're getting fat."

I choked back quiet tears as he ate his freshly cooked meal in front of me. I knew that if I cried too loudly, he would get even angrier.

"I'm sorry, Austin," I apologized. "I know that this is my fault. I'll tell him not to come around anymore."

"You do that, or else." He squeezed my chin with one hand. "This *is* your fault. You made me punish you. If you weren't so stupid, you'd realize what you're doing when you disobey me. Go to bed, I don't want to look at your pathetic face any more tonight."

The next morning Austin was still at home which made the hairs on the back of my neck stand on end. I walked downstairs to get breakfast. I made myself a bowl of cereal only for him to take it from me.

"Who said you could come downstairs?"

"What?"

"Did I come get you?"

"No."

"Then get back upstairs, I'll come get you when I decide you're allowed down here."

"Can I take my cereal?"

He grabbed me by my throat, "Did I say you can take your cereal?"

"No," my voice shook.

He released me. "Then get your ass upstairs. And if I hear you crying—don't let me hear you fucking crying!"

I ran upstairs, shutting the door behind me. I threw myself onto the bed, crying as quietly as I could. Why was he home? Shouldn't he be at work? I lay there for what felt like an entire day. My stomach growled and I began to get a headache from lack of food. Finally, I gave in and ate the ridiculous half slice of bread from the night before. Around four, I heard his feet clomping up the stairs.

"Get dressed, I made dinner," he ordered.

I got up, hoping it was something edible and something more than a piece of bread. I walked downstairs to see the table set. He actually did make dinner. I waited for him to tell me to sit down before eating. When he did, I tried to eat slowly so I didn't get a stomachache, but I was starving. He barely gave me a full portion of food.

"Tell me what happened yesterday," he said. "I know you were upset about that blonde, but that doesn't give you the right to disobey me."

"I'm sorry, I didn't intend to hang out with him. I was talking to Grace and he just joined us. I didn't want to be rude and tell him to go away. I'm sorry," I stated. "You cheated on me, Austin. I can't just forgive you and pretend like it didn't happen."

"I'm telling you now, I don't want you seeing him anymore. I don't like him." He ignored my later statement.

"But why?"

"I don't have to explain myself to you, I said stay away from him, so that is what you're going to do."

"He's my friend."

I regretted saying it the second it came out of my mouth. He stopped chewing his food, taken aback by my declaration. Slowly he lowered his fork down to his plate, staring at me with wide eyes. I braced for impact. He yanked me from my seat, shoving me into the kitchen cabinet.

"What did you say?"

I paused, thinking that not saying anything would work to help calm him down. But it only made things worse. He pulled me to him, shoving me against the cabinet even harder.

"I asked you a question!"

"I'm sorry," I blurted out in pain.

That sent him over the edge. He threw a punch trying to hit anything he could. He met my stomach, making it hurt so bad I thought I was going to throw up everything I had just eaten. I pushed him away as he swung his arm back for another hit, running up the stairs. My feet couldn't move fast enough. I fumbled over a few steps, hearing him behind me. I made it to the top and into the room. When I turned to shut the door, he threw his body weight against it, shoving it back into me. Grabbing a handful of my hair, he threw me into the closet doors. The force was so powerful that one of the doors fell off its hinges. I fell onto my knees as it toppled over on to me. I tried to get up, but didn't have enough energy to push it off me. He pulled me to my feet by my arm.

"Let me tell you something, you don't have any friends. Max—that loser—is gone. Now all you have is me. You know I'm the only one in the world who would put up with your shit."

I started to cry harder. He was wrong, wasn't he? As I stood there, I thought about all the ways I could get him to calm down. But saying nothing only made him think I wasn't paying attention to him. He kicked my feet out from under me. I fell backward, smacking my head against the wood floor of the bedroom. I crawled to the top of the stairs, praying for it to be over. Next thing I knew, Austin had me by the neck.

"Did you want to go back downstairs?" His lips pulled back to show his teeth in a vicious grin, like a predator toying with his prey.

"N—no," I choked out, knowing what he was going to do next.

"I think you do. I don't think you've learned your lesson."

He launched me into the air toward the stairs. I hit the wood stairs halfway down, falling straight onto my shoulder. I tumbled backward down the rest of the stairs. At the bottom I lay there, my entire body pulsing in pain. He walked down the stairs slowly, watching me carefully. When he bent down toward me, he snickered.

"Looks like you hurt your shoulder pretty bad," he taunted.

My shoulder looked almost like it was out of place. I met his eyes, begging for help.

"Have you learned your lesson?"

I nodded. "I'm sorry, Austin. You're right. He's not my friend."

If he wanted me to stay away from Damon, then that's what I'd do. As long as he didn't hurt me anymore, I would agree to cut anyone out of my life. He got me to my feet, helping me to the front door, as if I'd done this to myself. He handed me my keys, then pushed me out of the house.

"Straight to the clinic, straight back, or you may end up back there again," he threatened.

"I understand," I mumbled through an already swelling jaw.

I started the walk to the clinic. Halfway there, I was no longer crying, but I was in a lot of pain. I cradled my arm against my stomach so it wouldn't hang there, limp and useless. When I arrived at the clinic, I read the sign on the door. *Closed, in case of emergency dial 911.* Great, now what do I do? I couldn't call Max, he was gone. I didn't dare call Damon or Austin. I glanced back down the road, seeing the hanging sign for the coffee shop. Alex. I could call her at the coffee shop. I pulled my phone from my back pocket.

"Corner coffee," a man answered.

"Uh-hi, is Alex there?"

"No, she left for the day today. Can I take a message?"

"N-no that's okay. Thank you anyway."

I pulled my lower lip between my teeth, staring at my phone screen. The only person I could think of that was left was Grace. Maybe she could help me. I leaned against the wall of the clinic as I pleaded for her to answer.

"Hello?"

"Hey, Grace, it's Noelle."

"Hey, girl, what's up? Are you okay, you sound upset?"

"I um...I hurt my shoulder pretty bad and the clinic is closed. I'm not sure what to do."

"Where are you right now?"

"Still outside the clinic."

"Head to your store, I'll meet you and we can figure out what to do from there."

"All right, thank you."

I limped to the store and waited inside. Hearing her knock on the back door, I opened it and began to panic—Damon and Giovanni were right behind her. If Austin walked by, he would see us, so I closed the door that separated the front of the store to the back. Each of them walked past me, their eyes scanning my body. I still didn't know how bad I looked, but I could tell from their faces that this was not something I'd be able to cover up with a little extra makeup.

Damon had something in his hand.

"Jesus, sweetie. Did you get hit by a truck?" Grace asked, as she led me over to sit on the desk. I tried to laugh like it was all a big joke, but as my gaze bounced between the three of them, no one was smiling. "Come on, let's take a look at that shoulder.

I sat there as they examined my arm, worried about what could come from this situation.

"They are going to put your shoulder back in place," Grace explained.

"You know how?" I asked wearily.

They nodded, telling me to sit as still as possible. I did as they said. Damon touched my wrist lightly. When he placed his other hand on my bicep, he paused.

"Ready?" he asked.

"I guess."

"Okay, try to relax and don't move."

He pulled my arm slowly out to the side. He lifted it slightly before slowly pushing my bicep up and forward. I turned my body with the force he was using, causing him to stop.

"Noelle, you can't move, you have to sit still."

"That hurts."

"It won't once it's back in place." He looked at Giovanni, saying something in Italian.

Giovanni walked behind me, putting his hands on my shoulders near my neck. Damon did it again, slowly. This time I couldn't turn my body as Giovanni squeezed tightly, preventing me from moving. I heard a pop, then the pain lessened dramatically. Damon pulled something out from his back pocket. It was a sling. He cradled my arm in it, meeting my eyes for only a flash of a second as he carefully tightened the straps so it would fit me correctly.

"You should probably still go to the doctor tomorrow, just to make sure you didn't tear anything," Giovanni suggested.

"How did it happen?" Damon asked.

"I—I fell down the stairs at home."

There was a silence that fell over the room. It was like Damon wanted to say something more, but not with Grace and Giovanni there. Grace must have caught on.

"Come on, Gio, let's wait outside."

Once the back door shut behind them, Damon sat down next to me.

"Where were you today?" he asked, worried.

"I was at home. Austin was off so he made me—I mean, I decided to stay home with him," I sighed. "He doesn't want me seeing you anymore," I admitted. "He told me to stay away from you."

"What do *you* want?" he asked softly.

I laughed a little. "I just want friends. I want a normal life where I can hang out and have some fun. But that's not realistic."

"Why not?"

"Austin won't let it happen. I just don't think we can hang out anymore. I'm sorry, Damon." I looked down at my feet.

"Come on, Noelle, that's bullshit. Why are you letting him decide who you can and can't hang out with?" He paused, sighing. "I'm sorry, I just—what if he didn't know? There has to be a place where he won't cross paths with us." His eyes squinted as his eyebrows pulled together, "Why hasn't he shown up to the clearing? He's shown up everywhere else."

"He doesn't know I go up there, he never has. I wait until he goes to work in the city to leave for a run. That's part of the reason I run in the mornings."

"He works in the city? What does he do?"

"He drives a truck for some company, I think it's called Montero something."

"Andres Montero?" asked Damon. "Is Austin's last name Pierce?"

"Yeah, how do you—I mean, do you know him?"

"I know *of* him, that's all. I've heard his name before." He laughed a little. "Do you know what that company does?"

"No, I just know he works a lot. He only gets one day off every couple of weeks."

"So, then he won't find out if I see you in the mornings at the clearing. Let's start there. We can figure something out. Don't let him decide what you do, do what makes you happy."

I bit my lip, debating. He really wanted to see me. Plus, he did make me smile. He made me feel adventurous, like I used to be. Like I was with Max. But if Austin found out, I'd be in worse trouble. But he had no idea I went up there every morning. It wasn't like I was cheating on him. I just wanted friends.

"Okay," I finally agreed. "But he can't find out."

"Deal."

Just then, I got a call from Austin. I knew better than to ignore it. When I answered, I could tell he was still mad.

"Why are you at your store? I tracked your phone. The doctor's office is closed. Who are you there with?"

"I'm here with Grace and her husband."

"Oh, really. Come let me in, I'm out front."

"All right."

I hung up, turning to Damon. "You have to go. Austin is here."

He nodded, going out the back. I asked Grace and Giovanni to stay in the back as I walked up front to let Austin in. He charged toward the back room, relaxing when he saw I was telling the truth. He stuck out his hand to Giovanni, introducing himself. Giovanni took one look at his hand and clenched his jaw.

"You put your hands on my wife yesterday." He growled.

Austin turned to Grace, "My apologies, last time we met was not on the best terms."

Giovanni stepped towards him, half-blocking Grace from Austin's sight.

"Let me be crystal fucking clear with you. If you so much as touch another hair on her head you won't be alive to do it again."

"I understand, again I apologize. I'd had a rough day, which doesn't excuse my actions but know I truly am sorry."

I was confused as to why he was putting on such an act for them.

"You helped Noelle?" he asked Giovanni.

"Yeah, I dislocated my shoulder last year. Noelle called Grace when she saw the clinic was closed and we met her here. She should be fine. I put her shoulder back in place, but she needs to see the doctor tomorrow just to be sure it's going to heal correctly."

Austin nodded. "Thank god, I was worried." He reached out, running his hand down the back of my head.

I didn't say anything, just looked anywhere but at him. Grace suggested they get home. As we walked out the front door they stopped by a motorcycle. I looked at it, wondering if Damon had one. As we were walking down the street, I heard it rip away.

At home, Austin got me some ice for my shoulder and I took two Tylenol. He kissed my cheek.

"They were kind to help you," he said. "Grace is your friend?"

I looked at him, trying to figure out if this was a trick question. I decided to take it straight, giving an indefinite answer by shrugging my shoulders.

"I think if it's just you two, I'd be fine with you having some girl time. Maybe that will get your mind off being with someone else."

"I didn't think about being with someone else, you did."

"Then why did I catch you with Damon at the coffee shop yesterday, even after I made it clear I didn't want him near you?"

"He was just—he just showed up. I can't kick him out. It's a public place. You don't expect me to kick him out of the bar—it's the same concept."

"He didn't look like he was getting coffee," he snapped.

"He wasn't, he was talking to Grace."

"They know each other?"

"Grace is his sister-in-law," I said quietly. "Giovanni is his brother."

"What's their last name?"

This *had* to be a trick. He became furious when I knew Damon's first name. I shrugged my shoulders. "I don't know. I told you I don't know him that well. He is just a customer at the bar."

My lie worked. Austin believed me. I was unsure why he was in a better mood; maybe beating me made him more relaxed. Maybe it was the fact that I agreed not to see Damon anymore. I was unsure, but I wasn't complaining. He sat there quietly for a minute. The doorbell rang. I looked to see who it was as he got up. I smelled it before he said anything.

"Pizza. You must be hungry," he said, as if I was the one who was starving myself, not him. "I thought we could watch a movie or something."

I was so hungry, I agreed. I didn't know why he was happy with me one minute and crazy angry the next. Deep down, I knew in the end I needed to get out of this relationship. I didn't know how many more beatings I could take before my body gave up. And I didn't know how many times he cheated on me before I caught him. Or whoever had sent me the pictures caught him.

The rest of the night went by without incident. Although it was hard to sleep with my shoulder still sore, I managed to get a few hours in before Austin kissed me goodbye and left for work the next morning.

Chapter **Seven**

IT WAS HARDER TO GET DRESSED THAN I THOUGHT, AS I couldn't quite lift my arm over my head without it hurting. I Googled if I could run or not, and everything I read said it was all right, just no exercise involving my shoulder. It took me a bit longer than normal to get to the clearing as my body ached with each step. My breaths felt heavier. Halfway there I was on the verge of turning back, but then decided against it. The clearing was my peaceful place and I craved that. Especially after the past few days.

Grace, Giovanni, and Damon met me there, like our almost normal routine. Damon didn't hesitate to ask about my injury.

"It's better, but still sore. It was really hard getting dressed," I admitted, laughing at myself.

"Well, if you need help...you know, getting dressed or undressed, I can help," Damon smirked.

"Hmmm, I think I'd rather feel the pain," I joked.

Grace laughed, saying, "That's a first."

I looked at her, confused, remembering Giovanni saying that same thing the night I met them. I wondered why they would say that. Before I could ask, Giovanni caught my attention.

"Damon said Austin works for Andres Montero in the city."

"Yeah, why?"

"Did he say anything about us?" he asked.

"He asked me what your last name was, but I told him I didn't know."

"But you do know," Damon said confused.

"Yes, but then that would give him the impression you are more than a customer, which he doesn't want. But he apparently is fine with me hanging out with Grace."

"Why?" she asked.

I shrugged. "Because you are a woman. I guess."

"Sweet! First new girlfriend." She gave me a high-five, smiling.

"Ready for coffee?" I asked her, feeding off of her pleasant mood.

"Yep."

After coffee I went home to get cleaned up from the run. It was difficult getting undressed and even more difficult taking a shower. I did my best before going to the doctor's office. The doctor did a few quick checks of my injury, and then took an X-ray.

"Whoever put your shoulder back in place knew what they were doing," the doctor remarked. "Nothing looks permanently damaged, as long as you keep taking care of it. You can stop wearing the sling in a couple days. But I'll want you to follow up afterward."

I agreed to come back in a few days and went to open the store. I was busy until about two in the afternoon. When it was slow, I began thinking about Austin. His violent behavior towards me was getting worse. He'd never injured me so bad that I had to go to the clinic for help. There was no question that I had to leave, but how could I get out of that house? Until my arm was healed, I couldn't move boxes into the apartment above. Why couldn't we just talk things out? But would I change my mind if he talked to me? No. If I stayed, he would kill me. There was no denying it. As Grace came into the store, I tried to give her a half smile, but a tear escaped before I could turn away.

"What's wrong?" she asked, sounding alarmed.

"I'm just, I'm a mess, Grace. I don't know what I'm doing anymore."

"What do you mean?"

I pulled up the photos of Austin and that woman, showing her.

"Isn't that—"

"Yeah, it's Austin," I sighed, setting the phone back down.

"What did he say when you confronted him?"

"At first, he said he was sorry—she didn't mean anything to him and that he loved me," I tried to catch my breath. "But when I said he was only sorry he got caught, he blamed it on me. He said if I would have," I paused, trying to find a delicate way to say it. "Given more of myself to him, you know, then he wouldn't have to go find it somewhere else."

"He said that?" she asked in disbelief. "And you are still with him?"

I shrugged. "I don't know what to do."

She sighed. "Well, you have two options—either stay with him and try to reconcile, or leave him. I would only reconcile if you knew that he wouldn't do it again. But it's up to you."

I put my face in my hands. She softly touched my arm, trying to give me some comfort.

"Do you still love him?" she asked softly.

I shook my head. "I don't know what that means anymore."

A customer came in just then. Grace turned, saying hello for me.

"Go sit in back for a minute, I'll hold down the fort for a while."

As I sat in the back, I thought about what I would do if Max were here. After what happened yesterday, I think I would have told him the truth so he could help me get out. But Max wasn't here now. There was Grace, but she would tell Damon and Giovanni. If she told them, would I be able to survive the fallout with Austin? Then I could move on and take control of my life. I could unleash that sassy Noelle who was up for anything. Find someone that looks at me like Giovanni looks at Grace, with such yearning it would make me feel giddy inside. He'd stand up for me even when he knew I could stand up for myself. He'd do it not because I wasn't strong enough, but to show me I didn't have to stand on my own. I sighed, shaking away my daydream. Right now, it wasn't worth the risk to tell anyone. I was leaving him, no one needed to know the reasoning behind it. Besides, Grace will probably deduce it's because he cheated—as if I even needed more of a reason than that.

I closed the store a little early since I had a shift at the bar. Grace stayed with me the whole time. She walked home with me, offering to help me change. I hesitated at the front door, my mind going through the condition of the house. Austin would not be happy if I had someone over and the house was a mess. I didn't think so offhand, but she'd see me then, my bare skin, my scars. They were covered by bruises now.

"I think I'm okay to change, but you can come in if you'd like."

Her eyes softened, "I'd love to. I can even walk you to work."

I pushed open the door, stepping aside to let her in.

"Do you want a water or anything?"

"Oh no, I'm fine. Thank you."

"The living room is right there, make yourself at home. I'll be down in a few minutes."

It was so hard to get dressed, I almost called Grace to come up and help me. But I managed on my own, even if it took longer than the few minutes I'd promised her. She didn't mention it when I came back down, and she was quiet as we walked down the street towards the bar. "You know," she finally said, "whatever you choose to do is your decision and I can help anytime."

"Thanks, I just—" I paused. Someone like her, in a great relationship with family all around her, she wouldn't understand. "Don't know what I'm going to do right now. I guess I'll try to talk to him later tonight."

It was hard to serve with one arm down. I couldn't keep up with the drink orders. Finally, I took the damn sling off and shoved it into my apron pocket. My arm was weak, but it was better than fumbling around spilling drinks on people all night.

Three hours into my shift, I started feeling the pain more with each drink I served.

I was surprised when Grace and the guys came in, sitting down in their usual spot. As I served them, Grace held her hand out to me.

"What happened to your sling?"

"I can't keep up with it on, so I just took it off."

"Noelle, you are going to make it worse. You need to put that back on," Damon insisted.

I sighed, sliding it back on. My shoulder started to feel better as it rested against me. I stopped in the back and took some medicine for the pain. William called Madison in to help me out behind the bar. I was relieved. It was much easier with only half the people to serve. Austin came in after his shift in the city. He greeted me with a kiss on the cheek as I gave him something to drink. I wanted to push him away from me. During my break, I sat down in the back corner all by myself. Austin got up, sliding in next to me.

"What's wrong?" he whispered to me.

I looked at him. "Honestly?"

"Yeah, tell me."

"Every time I look at you, all I see are those pictures. My shoulder is seriously hurt and you were the one that did it, Austin.' I lowered my voice, "You threw me down the stairs."

Part of me was nervous, as I knew bringing it up might poke the beast inside him. But I had to make him aware that it wasn't okay. My muscles tensed as I braced myself for his reaction. He put his head on my good shoulder, hugging me lightly. When he looked up, he was crying. This was something I had never seen him do.

"I'm sorry, Noelle. I'll never do it again," he sniffled. "I love you so much."

He sounded genuine. I wiped his tears away with my thumb. My heart broke into two pieces. He was being honest, but I was still raw from it all.

"What do you want me to do?" he asked. "How can I prove it to you?"

"I just need time, Austin. I need to sleep on the couch or something so I can sort it out."

"Can I stay here for a bit or would you like me to go home?"

Who was he right now? I felt bad—I could tell how hurt he was by his voice.

"You can stay, it's okay...but my break is over."

He nodded, moving to let me out. He squeezed my hand before returning to his spot at the bar. I finished out my shift, wondering the entire time if Austin would flip his mood when we got into the house. He was waiting outside for me until I closed the bar.

"Ready to go?"

I gave him a half-smile. On the walk home, he put his arm around my waist. I didn't tell him to get off or push him away, but I didn't let him do anything else. I needed this night on my own to figure out what I was going to do. Once we got home, he brought me a pillow, a blanket, and ice for my shoulder.

Placing one hand on my cheek, he whispered, "I love you, Noelle."

He didn't wait for me to say it back. Instead, he got up, shut all the lights off, and went to bed. All night, I couldn't sleep. I could only think of what would happen if I chose to leave him. Was he being understanding now because he thinks it'll help me forgive him? If I stayed, I would be miserable or dead in a month. It was a major decision, stay and put up with him or try to leave and deal with the consequences. I had to leave. I shut my eyes, trying to find peace in my dreams.

The next three days felt like a blur. I was numb all over, thinking about my next move. I met Damon at the clearing each day, but that was the only time a real smile crossed my face. My shoulder was healing nicely and the doctor said I could begin using my arm for lighter things. This meant no more sling, which made me feel better.

Austin was trying to be nice, but it started to feel fake. Especially compared to Damon, who I was beginning to feel more comfortable with, during all the time we'd been spending together. He wasn't faking it; he was *actually* nice. But more than that, he was caring, thoughtful—real.

I'd made up my mind. I didn't want to be with someone who cheated and abused me. That night after dinner, I sat down to talk to him.

"Austin, I—I can't do this anymore."

"Do what?" he said, confused.

"I don't want to be with you anymore."

"Who do you want to be with? Damon?"

"He has nothing to do with this. You cheated on me, that right there shows me you don't really love me anymore."

"It *is* him and I do love you. Why are you so stupid, can't you see?"

I got up from the couch, flustered. I wasn't going to let him confuse me this time. He followed me upstairs to the bedroom.

"I'll move my stuff out tomorrow," I told him.

Most times, I could tell something was coming. He would charge toward me or yell insults before he would lay a hand on me. But not this time. There was no hesitation as he punched me once in the chest, knocking the wind out of me. I heard him laugh as I braced for another punch.

"What did I tell you the last time you tried this shit?" He backed me into the corner, his dark eyes furious as they stared into mine. "Do you need me to prove it to you?"

"No, I'm sorry, Austin. I take it back, I'm sorry. It's all my fault."

"You're going to learn not to think about anyone else but me!" He yelled, "you stupid whore."

He dragged me downstairs into the kitchen. He grabbed a knife, just like he had before. Only this time, he sliced my wrist open in three horizontal lines. He held my wrist over the sink, watching as the blood poured from the cuts.

"You have no more friends. Not the *Amoretti* brothers. And not that bitch, Grace. You go to work, you come home. If you don't, you will regret it for the rest of your life."

I began to feel dizzy. I fell backward, smacking my head against the countertop on the way down.

I woke up in the clinic, my wrist wrapped tightly with gauze and surgical tape. I looked around to see Austin talking to the doctor in the hallway.

"I got home and found her in the kitchen. She was just lying there." He appeared to be on the verge of tears. "There was a knife next to her on the floor."

"Has she done anything like this before?"

"No, never."

"Has she been acting differently recently?"

"She, she's been kind of distant lately. More quiet than normal and secluding herself, I just thought she was upset with me about something."

The doctor put one hand on Austin's shoulder.

"It's okay, she's alive. This isn't your fault," he tells Austin. "Just keep your eye on her. If you notice anything again, talk to her about it. Try to get her to share what she is feeling with you instead of keeping it inside. That will help her feel not so alone to the point of wanting to choose suicide."

When they saw me awake, Austin continued to act like he cared for me, rushing to my side. He took my hand in his, kissing the backside of it.

The doctor came and stood by the bed. "Noelle, we are all here for you. I'm going to send you home with some resources and phone numbers. If you are ever feeling like this again, call. Talk to someone, whether it be Austin or myself or someone else you trust. There are many people that care for you."

My eyes flickered between the doctor and Austin. He gave my hand a squeeze—a nonverbal order to say something.

"I'm sorry."

Tears began to trickle down my cheeks. But I wasn't crying because I was sorry. I was crying because there was nothing more

I could say. I was stuck in a place where I was unable to tell anyone the truth. Austin had almost killed me because I wanted to leave him. There was no doubt he would hunt me down if I just disappeared into the apartment like planned. This town was too small to hide from him. Was I really going to be stuck with him and his beatings for the rest of my life, however long that might be? The doctor discharged me under Austin's supervision.

I waited later than usual to go on a run the next morning. Hoping Grace and the guys wouldn't be up there by that time was a lost cause. I ran through the trail, only to freeze when I saw Damon, alone, waiting on me. He must have seen the look on my face.

"I have to go," I said quickly.

As I turned, Damon grabbed my wrist. "Noelle, wait."

The gauze slid down, revealing the cuts on my wrist. Damon looked to me; his breath caught in his throat as his eyes grew larger. His brows drew together as he took a step closer to me, his arms reaching out like he wanted to hold me. But no, I couldn't let that happen. If I did, I was afraid I might never want him to let go.

So, I backed away, and tried to say something to erase the concern from his face. "It's not what it looks like—"

"Why?" he asked, not letting me finish, still coming closer.

"Please, just leave me alone," I cried, holding my wrist close to my body.

"Not until you tell me what was so bad you had to choose this over getting help."

"Help?" I laughed. "There's no help for me."

"Nothing is *that* bad."

"Don't act like you know what I'm going through," I snapped.

"I'm not, I'm just—I'm trying to make sense of your reasoning."

"That's the beauty of it all, you don't have to."

I turned, starting my run back home. I skipped out on the coffee, going home to shower. I put a sweater over my tank top to cover up the bandage from any customers. When I opened the store, Grace came in with a coffee.

"Here, and don't even think about kicking me out until you answer my questions," she said firmly, handing me the coffee.

"Grace, please, I don't want to talk about it."

"Okay, but, please, just one question," she said. "Is this about Max leaving and you feeling alone…or what Austin did?"

I stared over her shoulder, refusing to meet her eyes.

"That's what I thought."

"I didn't say anything," I stated.

"Your expression did. What can I do to help?"

"There's nothing you can do," I insisted. "I'll be fine."

"This, is not fine," she pointed toward my wrist. "You need help."

"I just want to be left alone," I explained. "Grace, I appreciate what you are trying to do, but please just leave."

"I'm not leaving, but I won't ask any more questions. I'll just be here in case you do want to talk about anything."

She began walking around the store, taking a book from one of the shelves and making herself at home on the back couches. The store fell to silence aside from the light music playing over the speaker. I decided to occupy my mind by stocking some new books that I'd gotten in. Lugging the box out front, I opened it.

"Want some help with that?" Grace asked.

I nodded, taking a load of the books to a nearby shelf. Grace set up a display for them on the front table. She still hadn't asked anything more and it was starting to make me want to talk to her about what was really happening.

Then Austin walked into the store. It was as if he could feel it in his bones. I turned to Grace, my face begging her to leave.

"Thanks for the help," I said to her, tears welling up in my eyes once more.

"Yeah, I'll see you later."

Austin held the door for her as she walked out. He waited until the door was shut behind her to turn to me.

"I got off early, close up the store."

"I can't, I'll lose money."

He took a step toward me. All the warning he'd offer me this time.

"Okay!" I shouted, "I'll close up." He stood there waiting as I locked up.

"After your shift at the bar tonight, you come straight home."

"Okay," I mumbled.

As we walked through the front door, Austin barked his orders: "Make lunch, I'm starving."

"Wait, you made me close up the store to make you lunch?" I asked in disbelief.

He slapped me across the face. "I don't need your disrespectful backtalk. Do as I say."

I felt the burn as I made him a turkey sandwich—something he could've easily done himself. He made me sit in the living room with him while he watched TV. I eventually got up to use the bathroom.

"Where do you think you're going?"

"To the bathroom."

"You didn't ask to get up."

My head fell and I sat back down next to him.

"Can I go to the bathroom?" I mumbled.

"Come straight back."

Humiliation. That's what I felt as an adult having to ask permission to use the bathroom in a house that I called home. I made sure to ask if it was okay before I got ready to go to the bar.

"I'm leaving now," I said from the door.

"What the fuck do you do before you go somewhere?" he snapped.

I walked over to him, bending down to kiss him like he wanted. He slapped my butt as I turned to leave. On the walk to the bar, I cried, openly sobbing, not caring who witnessed it, just trying to get it all out before my shift started. Walking in, I saw Damon, Giovanni, and Grace. I knew then it was going to be a long night.

Chapter **Eight**

I AVOIDED THEIR AREA OF THE BAR TOP UNTIL I HAD to take over for Madison on her break. It was about halfway through my shift, and the longest fifteen minutes of my life.

"If you came for answers, don't expect to get any," I advised them.

"We're here to show you we can help you," Grace explained.

"No, you can't." I laughed. "I told you already. You don't get it."

I served the rest of the orders before returning to them.

"So, explain it," Giovanni continued.

I leaned on the bar toward them. "Why? Give me one good reason why I should explain what I am going through to you. I barely know you three."

"Because we're worried about you," Grace admitted. "Noelle, what you did, there are better ways to handle what you have been through."

"What have I been through, please tell me," I asked, intrigued.

She looked between Damon and Giovanni, which told me she didn't tell them what I had confided to her.

"You didn't tell them?" I asked surprised.

"It's not my business to tell," she stated confused. She squinted. "Tell me, what was your decision, after thinking about everything?"

"To stay," I lied.

"Then why do that?" She pointed to my wrist.

"Like I said, you won't understand."

I turned away, seeing Madison walk in from her break. They stayed there all night. It was Madison's turn to lock up, so I left out the back, walking toward the street. Damon came around the corner before I made it into the light. He walked me toward the alley.

"Noelle, what are you going through? Explain it to me" he said, his eyes searching mine, as if an explanation was possible. "Please?"

It was too much—too honest, too intense—I had to look away. "Just forget about me."

"I can't." He rested one hand on either side of my head, leaning against the wall of the building. "Ever since I met you, I can't get you out of my mind. So, tell me, why can't I help you?"

"You just can't."

He moved his body closer to mine, so much so it gave me chills. The closer he got, the more exhilarated I felt.

"Yes, I can. Tell me how."

His face was inches from mine. I so badly wanted to confess

everything to him right there. But before I could even respond, my phone began to ring in my pocket. I knew it was Austin calling without needing to look. I was late, and in trouble.

"I have to go," I said feeling breathless.

I ducked under his arm, walking quickly toward the road. I texted Austin I was on my way.

"I'm not giving up, Noelle!" he called after me.

Damon caring about me so much made me crack the smallest hint of a smile. As I reached the front door, Austin met me at the bottom of the stairs.

"Why are you late?"

"It took us a while to clean up tonight."

He grabbed the back of my neck, dragging me upstairs. He threw me toward the bathroom.

"Go shower, you have ten minutes," he ordered.

I did as he said, getting out just as he was coming in to shut the water off on me. I got in my pajamas, and as I lay down on the bed, Austin straddled me, wrapping his hands firmly around my throat.

"Austin, please, don't."

"You were late. I told you—straight there, straight back. You should have called if you were running late."

"But—"

He squeezed my throat tightly, watching me as I struggled to breathe. Just as I could no longer take it, he released the pressure. I coughed, gasping for air. But when he didn't move, I knew that wasn't the end of it. He started to squeeze again—this time tighter.

The skin on my face felt prickly, like a thousand needles. I tried to hit him, but I could tell in his slight smile he was enjoying this. When he released me this time, I tried to roll over so he couldn't choke me anymore. His weight was too much. I could only turn halfway. He grabbed my arms, pinning them above my head with one hand. The abrupt force sending a shooting pain through my shoulder. He took his other hand, choking me again, this time squeezing my throat so tight and for so long, everything went black.

He was gone the next morning when I woke up. I walked into the bathroom, trying to remember what had happened the night before. And then I looked in the mirror. Fingerprint bruises on the sides of my neck. The skin surrounding each bruise was tender to the touch. I left my hair down to cover them.

Damon was the only one at the top of the clearing when I got there on my run. His back was to me, his gaze out on the clearing. I quickly continued my run without stopping to speak to him, going straight to the coffee shop. When I left, he was outside waiting on me.

"What are you doing?" I asked.

"Waiting."

"For what?"

"For the moment you are ready to tell me how I can help you."

"You're going to be waiting a while."

"That's okay. Just know I'm here."

I walked home, getting ready for the day. No one, out of the three of them, made an appearance at the store. I was glad they were staying away. It was hard enough not to talk to Damon each morning. His stubbornness was obvious but I could be just as stubborn, especially with my life on the line.

Later, Austin showed up at the bar with two of his work friends. I tried my best to ignore them, but he waved me over.

"This is Noelle." He smirked up at me, rubbing my lower back before patting my butt. "She can hook us up with some drinks, right babe?"

"Uh," I swallowed, putting on a small smile, "sure."

I took their order, heading back to the bar to fill it. I overheard them talking about Damon and Giovanni as I dropped their drinks off to them.

"Yeah, the Amoretti mafia," one of them said.

"You know how many people they've killed?" The other leaned in closer, continuing, "Has to be dozens."

The first one nodded. "I heard they torture people in the back of their businesses."

"Here's the article on an investigation on their family," he said, turning his phone toward Austin. "I think that's why they moved to your Podunk little town."

"Yeah," the other agreed. "It's still close enough to drive back and forth, but far enough away from the pressure. Don't you think?"

Did the rumors ever stop? I knew Austin brought his friends here to spread all the gossip about them in front of me. Why else would they drive all the way from the city? Maybe he was looking for a reaction from me. He wasn't going to get one; I was going to act like I didn't care, even when I wanted to roll my eyes and tell them to stop gossiping like old women. I didn't dare do that.

"I don't know," Austin said, looking at me. "What do you think, babe?"

"No idea," I said, before walking away.

I got off early, starting my walk home. Austin wasn't far behind me, staggering. It took him a while to shower as I lay in bed, hoping to fall asleep before he got out. I didn't want to lie next to him and I hated when he tried to love on me. He did just that when he got out. In fact, he kissed me, once, and then again.

"Austin, stop."

He didn't listen, pulling me against him, hard. I pushed him away, wanting to be anywhere but there in that moment. My heart began to race. He kissed my neck, letting his hand run down the side of my body. Sliding my bottoms off, he ran his hand back up to my shoulders.

"I said stop," I said louder.

He climbed on top of me, covering my mouth with one hand.

"You don't want me to find it somewhere else, then you give it up whenever I say. There is no more telling me no, I'm taking it when I want it."

I shook his hand loose. "No, Austin, please!"

I pushed his shoulders away from me. He punched me straight in the eye. He held my arms down, forcing himself inside me. I felt a sharp pain as he continued to shove himself inside of me. I lay there crying as he panted over me.

"You know you want this," he said breathlessly.

His breath smelled of alcohol, his body pushing against mine harder and harder. Kissing my neck, he let out one last breath, moaning into my ear. When he finished, he rolled off of me, going to sleep like it was nothing. I quietly cried myself to sleep, curling into a ball, holding my knees to my chest.

I woke up feeling like I had lost a part of myself. No matter how hard I scrubbed my body in the shower, I still felt disgusting, like I couldn't get clean. I stared at myself in the mirror, my eye swollen and purple from the night before. I felt like a useless piece of trash he just threw to the side. Even if I made it out of the relationship, who would want someone so damaged? What did I have left of myself to give to anyone else? I opened the bathroom cupboard, finding the pain meds the doctor prescribed for my shoulder. I put them in my pocket, throwing on clothes to walk to the store. It was past the time to open, so I was sure I had missed the rush.

I walked there like a zombie, numb all over, dead inside. I unlocked the door, flip the sign to OPEN, and I curled up on the back couch, hugging my knees to my chest. As I sat there in the silence, I began to think what would happen after my shift at the bar that night—I would go home and what? Have another beating? Be raped again? I couldn't go back to that. I reached down, feeling the outline of the bottle in my pocket. Everyone seemed to believe I had already tried to kill myself once. I thought about it all day, and it made me sick to my stomach.

At the bar that night, I moved around serving customers only by muscle memory. My interactions were limited to taking their orders and thanking them for their tips. A smiled never crossed my face, genuine or fake. Damon, along with Grace and Giovanni, came in an hour or so after my shift started.

"What happened to your eye?" Damon asked the second I turned to serve him.

I shrugged, "I bruised it."

"How?" Grace prodded deeper into my explanation.

I slid them their usual orders, wondering what it would hurt to tell them. Then again, if I didn't take the pills, they would know, and I'd be in big trouble with Austin for telling them in the first place.

"Doesn't matter," I stated blandly as I walked away.

"Something isn't right," I overheard Giovanni say as I turned my back.

I began to serve other customers, avoiding eye contact with them until I had to refill their drinks. I was glad when they didn't say anything else. I didn't speak to them either. I went in back for my break, taking a few of the pills to help my shoulder, which was starting to get sore. I put my hair up in a ponytail before going back behind the hot bar. Madison turned to me as I was grabbing a glass for a customer.

"Oh, my god, Noelle, what happened to your neck?" she asked, taken aback by the bruises. "First your eye and then your neck, are they on both sides?"

They weren't as dark as they were the day before, but they were still highly visible. I didn't care enough earlier to bother covering them with makeup. I looked at her and I found I had no words left inside of me to explain, so I just pulled my hair out of the ponytail, trying to cover them back up.

"I'm fine."

I knew if she saw them, so did everyone at the bar, including the three people I didn't want to know the most. I refused every urge to look at them. A few minutes later, I asked William if I could leave early. I felt every customer in the bar staring at me. It was like they could see right through me as their eyes pierced my skin. My boss gave me the okay to leave since we were slow that night. Grabbing a bottle of water on the way out, I began walking toward the trails.

Chapter **Nine**

THE DARKNESS DEEPENED UNDER THE TREE BRANCHES that hovered over the trails. I used my phone light to get to the top of the clearing. Moonlight danced on the water below in a soothing glow. I leaned on a boulder; it was comforting to have something to rest against. I shook my head, laughing aloud. This is what it had come to, I was getting comfort from a freaking rock. I twirled the pill bottle in my hand, looking vacantly out at the water. Stinging tears gathered in my eyes before silently falling down my cheeks. As I sat there, I knew only one thing for sure—I was *not* going back to Austin.

I read the label on the bottle: 'DO NOT exceed 4 pills within a 24-hour period.' I had already swallowed three at the bar. I tilted the bottle into my palm coaxing another one out. With a deep breath I slid it onto my tongue. There were six left in the bottle. I wondered if that would be enough. I poured them all into the palm of my hand.

"Noelle!"

I turned as Damon knocked the pills from my hand, causing them to drop into the water below.

"What are you doing?" he yelled, panicked. "How many did you take already?"

"Four."

He read the label, relaxing as he saw the dosage. I stood up planning to walk away, but Giovanni and Grace blocked my way. As I tried to walk around them, Giovanni moved in front of me.

"Noelle, talk to us. We just want to help," Grace stated.

"You can't help! How many times do I have to say it?"

"We can, just tell us what's going on."

"No. Leave me alone and stay away from me."

"We are your friends, you owe us an explanation," Grace said.

I walked straight to her, getting inches from her face, "I *owe* you nothing."

"How did you get the bruises on your neck?" she asked.

I snickered, rolling my eyes. "They appeared overnight."

I tried to walk away again.

"Really, because it looks like those are bruises left by fingers, almost like someone choked you. Is that why you cut your wrist?"

My feet halted as she spoke. I looked out to the water as tears overcame me. I couldn't say anything as she continued.

"I think you tried to kill yourself because of what Austin did. That's why you came out here tonight. You were going to take those pills to try it again in hopes no one would find you."

"You're wrong!" I turned back toward her, with my fists balled at my sides.

She didn't know what I was going through, but she sure thought she did. She walked closer to me.

"Am I? Then tell me, what is so bad in your life you have to attempt suicide twice?"

Giovanni must have seen the distraught look on my face as he reached to pull her away. But as he reached for her, I covered my head, ducking out of instinct. They went silent for only a moment as I backed away. Grace's face, hard and tense moments before softened as she took a step back to give me space.

"You may be ready to give up, but we won't. We are here for you, just tell us what's going on. We're not going to stop until we know you are all right."

I'd had it at that point. "Why can't you just leave me alone?" I yelled.

"Because we care!"

There was a silence that fell between us.

"He hits you, doesn't he?" Grace broke the silence. "Austin is the one who gave you all those bruises."

My eyes snapped to hers as fresh tears began to stain my cheeks. My knees buckled, but Grace caught me, sitting me down on the boulder. They came closer. Grace sat next to me, placing her hand on my back to rub it gently.

"Tell us what's been going on."

I pointed to the cut down my arm that was now almost a scar. "This was because I didn't call as I left the bar one night after my shift. The bruise I had around my ribs? He beat the life out of me because I knew Damon's first name. Then he cheated on me, blaming me because I wouldn't give it up to him whenever he wanted. When I tried to leave him, he told me he'd kill me—because if he couldn't have me, no one could. The day he came into the coffee shop and saw you and Damon, he burned me with a cigarette." I pointed to the burn on my arm. "He starved me all the next day. He threw me down the stairs when I told him Damon was my friend, that's really how I dislocated my shoulder. When I tried to end it again, he laughed at me, telling me no one wanted me. Then *he* cut my wrist to prove he would kill me if I left him.

"I didn't try to kill myself," I continued. "He did it. These bruises?" I pulled back my hair. "This was because I was late coming home. And last night, he tried to have sex with me. When I told him no, he punched me." I pointed to my eye, pausing as I took a deep breath, I knew this was the hardest part to get through. "He told me that I no longer had the option of telling him no, he was going to take it whenever he wanted it—and then he raped me."

I looked at Grace, as a single tear dropped down her cheek. I looked down at my phone vibrating in my hand. I let out a desperate laugh seeing Austin calling. I wiped my cheeks as I answered it on speaker.

"Noelle, you fucking bitch, you're late. Did I not make myself clear last time you were late? You're so stupid, I swear, you're lucky you have me 'cause who else would want your dumbass. I'm tired of you disobeying me all the fucking time. Get your sorry ass home now or I'll come drag you home."

"I'm coming," I cried, hanging up. "I'll see you tomorrow...or maybe I won't. Who knows what I'm walking into this time?" I started walking to the trailhead.

"Let us help you," Giovanni said. "You don't have to stay there any longer."

"What are you going to do?" I asked.

"I'm going to kill him," Damon stated, walking toward me.

I stopped him, beginning to panic. "No, he can't know I told you. He'll kill me if he finds out."

He looked at me. "He's never going to lay a hand on you again."

"How long will it take you to get your things out of there?" Grace asked quietly. "We could help you move out, tonight. Then you wouldn't have to deal with him anymore."

I looked between the three of them. They were actually serious about helping me.

"You don't understand, he knows where I would be moving my stuff. He is just going to wait until everybody leaves to come after me. Even if I went somewhere else, he tracks my phone to find me."

"We can protect you," Damon whispered, putting one hand on my cheek.

I felt a rush of electricity through my body. I was unsure if it was just adrenaline because I was debating letting them help, or because of the way his hand rested so softly on my cheek.

I looked to Damon. His eyes were fixed on mine. I felt my body start to tingle, finally understanding that it was him making me feel this way. At the same time, I was terrified of what could go wrong with the whole situation. What if they got into a fight or what if he tried to hurt me while I was there packing up my things?

"I'm scared," I admitted, my voice shaking. "I don't know what to do."

"Let us help."

I took a deep breath. "Oh god, he's going to kill me."

Damon grabbed my hand. "Don't worry about him."

He walked next to me down the trail. Once we were by the bar, Grace began the run home to get a car for us to fill with my stuff.

"I'm only going to need maybe ten minutes. Austin told me I had to leave all my other things in storage, which is the apartment above the bookstore," I said quietly.

"Seriously?" Damon asked.

Giovanni said something in Italian to Damon, then got on the phone. He was done with his conversation within a few minutes.

"Noelle, shut your phone off. You can get a new one tomorrow," Damon advised.

I did as he said, pushing the phone back into my pocket as we came up to the front porch. Grace pulled up, another car behind her.

"Do you want me to go in first?" Damon asked.

I shook my head.

I walked up the front steps, opening the door. As I stepped inside, Austin came out of nowhere, grabbing me by the neck, slamming me into the wall. Damon shoved him off of me like he weighed nothing. Austin tumbled backward, recovering quickly as he tried to process what was going on.

"Sorry we're late," Giovanni mocked him.

"What the fuck is this, Noelle?" Austin yelled.

I looked him straight in the eyes, praying that my voice wouldn't sound shaky.

"I'm leaving."

Damon turned to me. "You and Grace go pack your things."

I nodded as Grace walked with me up the stairs and into the bedroom.

"I am just going to take the stuff in the dresser. Let's just shcve everything in this suitcase. I want to get out of here as quickly as possible."

Fifteen minutes later, we were coming down the stairs. Damon met us halfway, taking the suitcase from me. He handed them to a guy I hadn't seen before.

"Who is he?"

"He works for us, he's here to help."

As I walked to the front door, Austin began yelling to me.

"You're dead, Noelle, you hear me? They can't protect you forever."

Damon turned, grabbing a handful of Austin's shirt. He pinned him against the wall.

"If you even come near her again, I will kill you," Damon threatened.

Giovanni spoke in Italian before Damon released Austin.

He walked toward me, turning back to Austin. "You're lucky I don't kill you now for what you've done."

Austin laughed darkly, "You don't have the balls."

Damon charged toward him. He slammed Austin against the wall again, and pulled out a gun from the waist of his pants and placed the barrel against Austin's head. I gasped, both of my hands flying to cover my mouth.

"Damon, calm down," Giovanni ordered.

I don't know what else he said since it was in Italian, but I did hear my name. Damon looked at me, and when he saw how scared I was, he put the gun away, walking toward me.

"That's what I thought. You Italian bastards don't have the balls to act on your threats." he taunted. "You can't stay with her forever. It won't take long for you to realize she's just a piece of shit you don't want either."

I saw Damon's fists ball up and his jaw clench.

"What, nothing to say now?" Austin laughed. "Just like that she made you go from threatening to pathetic because she's scared of a damn gun. It's going to be easier than I thought to get her alone. Then what are you going to do, Damon? Try to scare me with your empty threats?"

Damon turned, throwing a punch at Austin. His knuckles met the side of Austin's face, causing him to stumble backward, grasping at the railings of the stairs to keep from falling. Then he swung again with his other hand, knocking Austin down. It only reminded me of all the times I was at the end of the abuse and I felt more tears coming. Giovanni and the other man with them pulled Damon off of him. Grace walked me outside. I had to take big deep breaths to keep from throwing up. Austin was still yelling from the inside the house. Damon walked over minutes later; I jumped when he put his hand on the small of my back.

"I'm sorry, I didn't mean to scare you. Are you ready to go?"

"Yes, please."

The two guys in the second car went inside behind us as we left. Damon drove us to the bookstore, carrying my things up to the apartment. Grace helped me unpack until Giovanni got there.

"Do you want me to stay?" Damon asked. "I can sleep downstairs on the couch in the store, if you want."

I knew that Austin would come for me, but if Damon were there, I'd be safe, right? I nodded, saying goodbye to Grace and Giovanni as they left.

"Thank you," I whispered as we sat on the couch.

"Why didn't you tell us?" His voice was gentle, like he was afraid to ask.

I felt tears coming on again. My body was exhausted and I was tired of crying.

"I thought—I thought he loved me. Then, when things went downhill, I was—I was scared of what he would do if anyone found out. I'm sorry."

The tears were full-blown now. Damon scooted closer to me, wiping the tears from my cheeks.

"You have nothing to be sorry about, none of this is your fault. I don't care what bullshit he said to you, it is not your fault."

Reaching my arms around his neck, I leaned into him. He pulled me toward him, holding me tightly. Comfort washed over me as he lightly ran his fingers up and down my arm. I leaned my head on his shoulder, tucking it just below his chin. That night was the first night I fell asleep feeling safe, in his arms.

I awoke, screaming—I thought I had dreamed it all. I sighed, running my hands through my hair. Damon came in moments later.

"Are you okay?" he asked, turning on the light.

I looked around the room. I was in the bedroom, but I remembered falling asleep on the couch with him. He sat down on the edge of the bed.

"How did I get in here?" I asked, the confusion clear in my voice.

"You fell asleep, I was holding you. Don't you remember?"

"You carried me in here?"

"Yes."

Unsure as to why I was still confused, I continued to look around the room.

"I'm not dreaming?"

"No, you're not." He smiled a goofy smile. "Unless you *want* to dream about me. Then yes, this could be a dream."

He made me laugh ever so slightly. "Yep, this is real."

"Did you have a nightmare?"

I nodded seeing the visual of Austin coming at me with a knife, ready to kill me. His words from my dream echoing through my mind; *I told you I'd kill you if you tried to leave me.* He'd launched himself on top of me, jolting me awake. Not wanting to go into depth with Damon, I changed the subject. "You're not really sleeping downstairs in the store, are you?"

"Yes, I didn't want to make you uncomfortable."

"You can bring your stuff up here if you would like, I don't mind."

He did as I offered, moving from the couch downstairs to the one upstairs, closer to me. Knowing he was there, I slept through the night without another nightmare about Austin.

Chapter **Ten**

 to see if my senses were teasing me. Sure enough, I heard Damon talking on the phone as he cooked at the stove.

"I don't even know what to say, Giovanni..." he paused. "What if she doesn't want to? ...Fuck you," he laughed. "All right already, shit, I'll see you in a bit."

Going into the bathroom, I checked out my bruises in the mirror. The ones on my neck were better, but my eye looked terrible. Makeup was a definite necessity today to cover it up. Sighing, I walked out into the kitchen.

"Morning. You want some?" he asked.

"Sure, why not." I smiled, taking a plate.

We sat down, eating at the small circular table I had in the eat-in kitchen.

"Has anyone ever told you you're a great cook?" I asked him with my mouth full.

"Cooking is relaxing to me." He chuckled, his cheeks flushing. "How are you feeling this morning?"

"I'm fine." I turned my attention to the food on my plate.

"Okay, now tell me your real answer." He half-smiled. "Honestly, please?"

"My head hurts and I'm sore, nothing I can't handle though."

"Let me get you some Tylenol."

He stood up before I could protest. It was then I noticed a bag on the counter from the pharmacy down the street. He retrieved a bottle, dumping a couple into his palm before walking back to me.

"Here, one or two?"

I reached out, taking two from his hand and downing them with my orange juice.

"Thank you." My voice was soft.

"Anytime." He took a drink of his orange juice, clearing his throat, as he looked around the apartment. "Did you live here before?"

"Yeah, from the time after my parents' died to when I moved in with Austin. It wasn't a long time, but I made it my own while I lived here. It made me feel closer to my parents, somehow, since we all spent so much time together downstairs."

"Your dad visited your mom often?"

"Almost every day." I nodded. "After work he came by to pick her up. Which was really him helping her restock and order new books, closing stuff too. He'd even work on cases in the back room to keep my mom company on the days he worked from home." I smiled at the memory. "He would read the Italian version of Dante to me while I followed along in the English one."

"But he never taught you Italian?"

"I mean, I can sometimes pick certain words out of a story that I know, but they are all commonly used words. Hearing it is an entirely different story. Don't worry, you guys speak too fast for me to even figure out where the words are."

He chuckled. "I could teach you if you really wanted to learn."

"Maybe, once I'm situated." I grinned, taking my last bite.

"Yes, make sure you're situated. It will take a lot of late-night study sessions...if you know what I mean." He winked.

I rolled my eyes. "Okay Romeo, chill out."

He threw his hands up in mock offense.

"Hey! I'm just trying to support you in your journey of becoming an Italian speaker."

"I'm sure that's what you're doing."

I crumpled up my napkin, playfully tossing it at him. He didn't attempt to dodge it as it flew towards his chest, bouncing off back onto the table. I stood up, bringing my dishes to the sink. He did the same, helping me clean up the kitchen.

"Grace and Giovanni want to meet for coffee. Are you up for that?" he asked leaning back against the counter.

"Yeah."

We walked down to the coffee shop, picking a table as we waited for them to arrive.

"Do you have plans today?" he asked.

"Well, I was going to open the store, but after everything that happened last night, I think I'm just going to take the day off."

Grace's squeal interrupted Damon as he opened his mouth to

say something. She sat down across from me as Giovanni got them coffee before joining us.

"Are you coming, Noelle?" she asked.

"Coming where?" I turned to meet their eyes.

"You didn't ask her?" they said simultaneously to Damon.

"I was working up to it."

Giovanni crossed his arms. "Ask her now," he ordered.

Damon scratched the back of his head. "They want to know if you want to go to the city today. You can get a new phone there and then we can stay there for a bit."

"Really?" I let the excitement out in my voice. "I've haven't been to the city since I was little."

"Are you joking?" Grace asked in disbelief.

"No, my parents took me a few times, but not much, and I was young, five or six maybe. Plus, Austin wouldn't let me go or take me, for that matter."

"Well, that's settled then. You're coming with us today."

I was really excited, unable to contain it as we walked back toward the store. Giovanni and Grace started home at the corner. Damon followed me upstairs to the apartment.

"Aren't you going to shower and get ready?" I asked.

"I wasn't sure if you wanted to be alone or not."

"Good point, I'll be quick."

"If you need me to wash your back, let me know," he winked.

I giggled, "I'd rather have a dirty back."

"That hurts." He pointed to his heart. "Right here, you got me."

"Awww, poor Damon," I put my hand on his cheek. "It's still a no."

I jumped into the shower, quickly washing up. I threw on some makeup to cover the bruises. What do I wear? It was nice outside, so I put on jean shorts and a V-neck shirt. Coming out into the living room, I asked Damon if it was okay to wear. He stood up, walking over to me.

"You look amazing, as always." He smiled.

"Really?" I felt my smile widen. "Thanks."

Walking to his house, I couldn't stop looking over my shoulder, afraid of where Austin was at this point. Damon noticed, putting his hand on my back.

"You don't have to do that anymore. He's not going to hurt you again."

"I just—it's weird not to."

Damon lived in a huge house. It was the ultimate bachelor's pad. A laugh escaped my mouth.

"Damon, why do you live in such a big house if it's just you?"

"Well, I was assuming I'd have a family of my own one day," he said, laughing nervously.

"I guess that makes sense."

"The library is through those doors, or you can walk around. Explore. I'll be down in a bit."

I turned, opening the door down the hall to the library. It was huge and amazing. Finding something to read was easy and almost immediate. I got so sucked into the book I didn't hear anybody calling my name.

"Hello! Earth to Noelle."

Glancing up, I smiled at Grace.

"Ready?" she smiled.

I jumped up, setting the book on the table next to the couch. I walked up to the front door as Damon came down the stairs.

"Whose car are we taking?"

Giovanni looked to Grace. "Someone wants to take the Lambo."

"That means we'll have to take two cars," Damon said, looking at Grace. "All right, let's go then."

I followed him to the garage attached to the house. Damon had a Lamborghini as well. I looked at him.

"These are expensive cars."

"Yeah, but worth every penny." He paused, "I have an everyday car if you want to take that one." He pointed to a jeep behind me.

"Oh, no, we can take this one!" He opened the door for me. It opened upward instead of out to the side.

I laughed, "This is too much."

He got in, pulling out of his driveway. Giovanni and Grace were in the exact same car, just a different color. They tore out of the neighborhood.

Damon laughed to himself. "Hell, yeah." He looked to me. "Are you buckled?"

"Yes."

"Good, hold on."

He floored it, spinning the tires, catching up to Giovanni, then passing him. They continued to pass one another back and forth. I watched Damon's muscles flex as he shifted gears, unable to take my eyes off him. I thought back to that night I saw a tattoo on his chiseled chest, wondering what it really was. We drove out of town and onto a two-lane highway. Farmland surrounded our town. I assumed it was like that all the way to the city. But the farmland slowly turned into woods the further we drove. In the sunlight, it looked so calming and reminded me of the woods I walked through on the trails. Only these trees were twice the size of the ones in town and altogether covered more area. We passed an opening in the woods with a big field of flowers. My eyes were glued to the window as I took in the sights that passed. When I caught a glimpse of the tall buildings of the city in the near distance, butterflies started dancing in my stomach.

"Wow, look," I pointed to the buildings in the distance. "You can already see them from here."

Damon chuckled. "I can't wait to see your face when we get there."

Damon parked the car, and as we got out, he and Giovanni argued over who won the race there. I was too busy looking up at the tall buildings around me to care. They were huge, almost disappearing into the sky. There were people walking everywhere—some in business clothes, others in everyday street clothes. The street was four lanes wide—I couldn't remember seeing so many cars on one street before. Horns were sounding all around. It was so noisy, unlike town. If someone caused a ruckus, the entire town would hear, as it was normally a quiet place—with the exception of the summer cookout that involved everyone in town. Grace put her arm through mine.

"Come on, let's get you a phone. They will probably be out here all night if we let them."

I walked with her inside. Picking out a phone was easy, as I didn't care which phone I had. They transferred everything for me except the app Austin had downloaded to track my phone. The first thing I did was text Max my new number. I knew he wouldn't get it until he got home, but I was sure he would call me the second he could. The guys were still bickering about who won as we walked back to the cars.

"Noelle," Grace said softly, "I never apologized for pushing you so hard last night. But I want you to know that I did it so you would tell me what you were going through. I didn't mean to make you as upset as I did."

"I understand."

She gave me a hug before turning to the guys, butting in on their argument.

"Where to?" she asked.

They all looked at me. I threw my hands up.

"I don't know why you are looking at me, I've never been here as an adult to remember much!"

"Let's go get lunch, it's about that time," Giovanni glanced down at his watch. "Do you like sushi?"

"I've never had it," I admitted.

"Do you like fish?"

"The only fish I've had were salmon, shrimp, and tuna. I liked those but I haven't had any weird exotic kinds."

He laughed, then saw I wasn't joking.

"Oh my god, you are serious. Do you know what sushi is?"

"Yeah," I chuckled, "I have read about what sushi is. I said I've not been to the city in a long time. I'm pretty sure all I ate as a child was chicken nuggets. So, my fish experiences were limited to what I was brave enough to try to cook on my own."

Giovanni nodded, taking Grace's hand, "Let's go."

Damon walked beside me, putting his hands in his jean pockets. He cleared his throat before nudging me with his elbow.

"What?"

"If you don't like the sushi, we can go get pizza."

"Good plan, I'm not sure I'm going to like it. Raw fish is intimidating." He laughed and I watched him relax a little.

Inside the restaurant, I watched as the sushi chef created our meal behind the counter. It was interesting how fast he worked. It was like art, the way he shaped each piece and cut each roll. We sat down to eat, climbing into a booth.

"It's not bad!" I said, tasting it little piece at a time. "What's this?" I picked up a big blob of green stuff with my chopsticks, popping it into my mouth.

"Noelle, don't—" It was too late—my tongue was on fire.

"That's wasabi! It's very hot," Giovanni laughed. "Why didn't you wait for an answer before you tried it?"

"I don't know, I don't know!" I complained. "It burns!"

"It might help if you kiss me." Damon smiled.

I looked at him through squinted eyes, "I'd rather let my tongue burn off."

"Wow, I like her," Grace laughed, "That's only the third time that's happened. And, if I may point out, the first time it happened was *also* with her."

I took a drink of my soda, trying to get my tongue to cool off. "What does that mean?"

"You are the only woman who has ever stood up to him or flat out denied him. He normally gets this," she cleared her throat and began speaking in an overly girly tone. "Oh, Damon, whatever you want, take me home, I love you."

"So, I'm confused," I laughed. "If you're so irresistible, why don't you have a girlfriend already?"

He shrugged like it was no big deal. "I haven't met the right one."

"They either want the name or the money," Grace explained.

I rolled my eyes, "Money is not everything, and no offense, but what is the importance of your name?"

"Our family is very well-respected and prominent in the city," Damon answered. "Taking our last name would include someone in that."

"Oh, I see." I didn't really, though.

"Just wait," Grace assured me., "We can go to the club tonight and you'll see it firsthand."

We walked after lunch, just looking around and stopping at a couple stores. Then I spotted a lovely water fountain in one of the parks. It was made of stone, and people were sitting on the outer edge. I stopped a few feet in front of it, admiring the chiseled lines making it appear to be an oversized chalice.

"What attracted you to this?" Damon asked.

"I like how detailed it is."

"Do you like sculptures?"

"Yeah, but I've only seen them in books."

He smiled, extending his arm to me. "Come with me."

I laced my arm through his, walking around to the other side of the park to a circular cement clearing. It had benches around the outer edge and in the middle was a giant glass cube set up on a point. The light from the sun shone through it, making a rainbow appear on the ground.

"Wow," I breathed, smiling. "That's beautiful."

"There's a ton of artwork throughout the city. I'm sure we can see more as we walk around today."

"They are all over? Not just at the parks?"

"No, there are some outside the courthouse, the baseball stadium. There's even an art district in the city as well."

My eyes widened. "I would love to see that!"

"Let's go find Grace and Giovanni. Then we can head over there."

The art district was more than I could have ever imagined. It started with a giant archway covered in flowers. There were sculptures on every corner and shops down the length of the street. Some antique stores and some art galleries. Grace and Giovanni walked slightly ahead of us. I watched as he reached out, taking his hand in hers as she pointed out something up ahead.

"Look they are having a showing!" her eyes sparked with amusement.

Giovanni groaned, "We'll be in there for hours if you step through that door."

She giggled. "Then I guess you'll be pretending to like art for hours, just to humor me."

"You got that right." He leaned over, kissing her temple as we waited to cross the street.

We followed them through the crowd of people walking around just as we were. Giovanni opened the door, stepping in and then to the side for Grace to pass through. She was immediately drawn to a painting on the wall, pulling him by the arm to join her. Damon chuckled behind me and my eyes danced across the room. There were paintings on the walls, sculptures around the room, some small enough to have in your home. Others were large, needing the area with the higher ceiling to be placed inside the building. There was calming piano music playing in the background that entwined with the quiet conversations of the others around the room.

I joined Grace and Giovanni as they spoke with someone about the painting she was interested in. It was filled with splashes of different shades of red and pink with harsh lines of black around the outside of it. A round of abrupt laughter caused me to glace over, my eyes catching on a tiny sculpture in the next room over. As to not interrupt anyone I quietly stepped away, heading towards the sculpture like it was calling me to it. There was a little plaque next to it reading: *Tenacity by Harold J. Bowen*

It was of a small elephant trying to climb out of a mud pit. The elephant itself was white and shiny, having deep brown blotches on it resembling it's fall into the mud. The resonation I had with this little elephant made my heart pinch. There were times when I felt like that elephant, the hell I lived in attempting to swallow me whole as I struggled to get out. I found myself rooting for the elephant, willing it to move out of the mud with my mind. I bent down, getting close with it.

"You'll get there, little guy." I whispered.

"What drew you to this?"

I turned, meeting eyes with an older man. He was wearing a suit and had his hands tucked behind his back.

"I-I don't know."

"You seem attached to it already. Would you like to purchase it?"

"You can buy it?"

"Of course, all the art you see is for sale."

"How much is it?"

He pulled his arms forward, revealing a clipboard. He slid on the glasses that were in his suit jacket pocket before running his finger down the paper in front of him.

"That piece is...ahh, $7,497 pre-tax."

I almost choked on the air I'd inhaled. Seven thousand dollars! Thank goodness the rest of the gang walked over before I had a chance to answer to his question. Grace was smiling wide.

"Can I help you gentlemen?" the guy asked.

"Yeah, we'd like to purchase a canvas." Giovanni replied.

"Sure, which piece?"

"I'll lead the way!" Grace offered, spinning on her heal, a glint of excitement in her eyes.

Giovanni peered back at us, shaking his head with a smile.

"I don't even know where she's going to put this in the house."

Damon chuckled, "She'll find a place for it."

I turned back to the piece I'd been standing in front of.

"So, this is what you ran off to inspect?" He smiled.

"Oh-sorry-I—"

"You don't have to apologize, Noelle." His eyes flickered to the piece. "I would love to know what you're feeling though."

"I feel great."

"I mean when you look at that." He pointed to the little elephant.

"Oh..." I chewed my lower lip. "I guess I feel attached to it; the elephant I mean. It's just trying to get out even though it's been almost engulfed in the mud. It's like the mud is trying to hold onto her. I can feel her struggle—I mean, it, the *elephant's* struggle," I corrected myself. "And...I'm rooting for it, I guess. What do you think about it?"

"Elephants are a symbol of strength you know." He noted, "and it's white, which is a symbol of purity. I think this is showing that you can overcome anything with your inner strength. No matter what's trying to bring it down, it's going to rise above it all."

The corners of my lips turned up as I raked my eyes over it once more. His interpretation of it was almost the opposite of mine. I was focused on the mud whereas he was focused on the strength.

"Well, who knew you weren't just a pretty face." I teased.

He let out a laugh, just as Grace and Giovanni were coming back to join us.

"Ready?" Grace asked.

My head turned back to the sculpture, not quite ready to leave it.

"I think I'm going to be another minute."

"Oh no." Giovanni glanced at Grace.

"Well, that means we can go look in the other room at the sculptures." She tugged on his arm, "Think we should get one for the backyard?"

"Do I think we should get one? No. Do I feel as though you are going to find one? Yes."

I giggled as she pulled him behind her, beginning to explain why they needed a sculpture in their backyard. Damon hovered behind me for a few minutes before walking to look at a piece on the wall. I just kept admiring that little elephant. It wasn't until Grace and Giovanni came back that I finally decided I was okay to part with it forever. Damon rejoined us as we headed outside.

We spent the better part of the day there before starting the trek back to the cars. I couldn't take my eyes off the buildings as we passed them. They were so impressive. I heard Damon laugh as I stared up at a building as we waited for the crosswalk sign to change. It was a shorter building in comparison to the others around it, but with a string of lights and some sort of outdoor covering.

"What are you admiring?"

"Just trying to figure out what's up there," I said, pointing to the roof.

"That's probably a rooftop pool or something."

"Wow. Why put a pool on the roof?"

"So, you can enjoy the view of the city while you relax."

"Oh." I looked back up toward the top of the building, wondering what it looked like from above.

"Next time we come, I'll take you up there," he whispered.

"Really?"

"If you'd like."

My smile never faded as we walked to the cars. They drove to the other side of the city and we ate dinner at a restaurant they were familiar with. "Gelato for dessert?" Grace asked as we left the restaurant.

Giovanni smiled at her. "Anything you want." He gazed at her like she was his entire world. I wondered what it would feel like to have someone look at me that way. I looked down at the ground as we walked. Damon put his arm around my shoulders.

"You okay?" he asked.

"Yeah, I'm fine, I was just thinking."

"Want to talk about it?"

I shook my head, wondering what he would say if I told him. He dropped his arm from my shoulders, rubbing my back. The next store we went into looked like an ice cream shop.

"Ice cream?"

"No, gelato. It's just a little different," Damon explained.

We ordered, then found a booth. As Damon reached over to get some of mine, I slid it away.

"I don't share dessert," I teased.

"Don't you know him?" He pointed toward the door.

I looked up, but nobody was there. I quickly glanced back to see Damon sneaking a spoonful of my gelato. I squinted at him suspiciously, then sniffed near him.

"Your gelato smells weird."

"No, it doesn't. It's pistachio."

"Yes, it does, I smell it from here. Smell it for yourself."

He scooped up a big spoonful, bringing it to his nose. I pushed his spoon toward him, getting gelato all over his face. He laughed, wiping it away with a napkin.

"No one steals my dessert and gets away with it," I declared.

"All right, just wait, Noelle! I'll get you back."

"Doubt it," I snorted.

Finishing what we had left, we headed back toward the cars. Grace said we were going to the club she talked about earlier. I was part excited, part anxious. I had never been to a club.

Chapter **Eleven**

THERE WAS A LINE OF PEOPLE OUT THE DOOR AND down the block. I had never seen such an insanely long line to get into a club. Then again, I had never actually been to a club.

"You have to wait in that line to get in?" I questioned. "People actually wait that long?"

"We are going straight in through the red rope," Giovanni explained.

"Oh, because of your name," I assumed.

Damon laughed, "No, we are the owners."

The girls in the line began to scream Giovanni and Damon's names.

I laughed. "I think your fan club is here."

"Oh, just wait," Grace shouted over the commotion. "That's only the overflow of the fan club. Most of them are inside already, there's no doubt."

The guy at the door greeted them, unhooking the rope to let us through.

Inside, it was packed. We maneuvered through the crowd, sitting at the bar on the farthest side, away from the door. I looked around. I noticed at least six men in suits, their eyes scanning the crowd then looking toward us. I wondered how they could keep track of everyone.

"I think it'd be fun to bartend at a place this busy."

"You would definitely see it all here." Damon nodded.

"Hey, handsome," a young woman cooed, reaching for his bicep. "Don't you want to buy me a drink?"

I turned to Grace. "Do you think they can sniff him out?"

She rolled her eyes at the woman, and leaned closer to me. "Try dating him while that happens. It gets infuriating."

"Oh, I wouldn't doubt it."

Damon politely declined, and as the girl walked away, I turned to him.

"*Hey handsome,*" I said, doing my best to imitate the sultry tone of the woman Damon had sent away. "Wanna buy me a drink?" I finished, collapsing into laughter.

He grinned, but held up two fingers to the bartender, who nodded, and swiftly set two glasses on the bar in front of us.

"To new beginnings." Damon raised his glass toward me and I did the same, until they kissed in a gentle *clink*.

"To new beginnings," I repeated, something in me thawing under his watchful gaze.

"*Salute,*" he added, taking a long swig from his glass.

I did the same, unable to tear my eyes away from him. I finished my drink and set the glass down. He ordered me another. "Seriously, I still don't understand how you're single. All these girls in here falling all over you."

He smiled slightly. "I want someone who doesn't care about my name or money. I want someone who loves me for me and my charming personality."

Laughing, I took a sip from my drink. "Oh, yes, you can't forget about the charm. But, still, there has to be someone in here who meets your standards."

"I'm positive there is. Come dance with me?" He smiled a big, goofy grin. "Or wait, let me guess, you'd rather your legs fall off?"

I pulled him to his feet, lacing my fingers through his as I made my way onto the dance floor. His hands moved down my arms, resting on my hips. He pulled me close to him as we danced. The music just fast enough for me to follow as I was not the best dancer. Having two left feet would be an understatement when describing my dancing abilities. Damon didn't seem to mind as he kept dancing right along with me until the song ended. I felt my entire body tingle as he leaned into my ear.

"You are the most beautiful woman here."

His breath on my skin gave me chills. The DJ took a break shortly after that, letting a track play on its own. We pushed through all the bodies to get to a booth along the back wall. A guy walked up, setting a drink down for Damon.

"Do you want something?" he offered.

"No, I'm good for now."

The guy walked away, leaving just us two.

"Thanks for bringing me to the city." I smiled. "It's amazing! Well, what I have seen of it."

"Anytime you want to come, let me know."

"Can I ask you a question?" I felt nervous asking him, but I wanted to know. He nodded.

"Do you run the club? Like, is that your job?"

"Yeah, we run this one and we own another club on the other side of town as well. There's really nothing special about it."

"Then why is your family so prominent?"

"We're involved in the community. We help the city rejuvenate areas that are more run down. My family has money, so we use it to help those who might need it. We are the leading business in the city because we are involved in both the business and community. The guy Austin works for has the second spot. He wants our position, obviously, so it can get dangerous."

"What does that mean, exactly?"

He sighed. "It's hard to explain."

"That's all right, I was just being nosy anyway."

"Hey, I know a place you will fit right in."

I laughed, shaking my head as he scooted toward me, putting his arm on the back of the booth. I moved closer, gazing into his eyes. A young woman slid into the booth, interrupting the silence between us.

"Damon!" she squealed, like she was an old friend.

He didn't look away from me, ignoring her. But his eyes showed exactly how annoyed he was. I smiled at him before turning to her.

"Can I help you?"

"I was talking to Damon. It doesn't concern you."

"He's busy, can I take a message?" I smiled.

She looked at me, offended, getting angry as Damon let out a laugh.

"Listen, bitch," she came back at me. "Like I said, this doesn't concern you. You are lucky he is giving you the time of day. There are way more girls in here that are prettier and a hell of a lot more sophisticated than you."

She stood up, leaning down into my face.

"Hey, take it easy," Damon said to her. But I slid out of the booth and stood very close to her, eye to eye. I was ready to throw down right there. What was coming over me? I was tired of being a victim. Sooner or later, I had to take a stand, right? Just like that damn little elephant. The liquid courage I had been drinking over the previous two hours may have also been a factor. I had gotten into fights when I was in school with other girls and they didn't intimidate me. Not like guys did. She pushed my shoulder backward with the tips of her fingers.

"Move out of my way," she ordered.

I took another step closer. "Touch me again and you will regret it."

Damon put his arms around me from behind. "Come on, Noelle."

He walked me away from the girl. Leaning against the back wall next to a standing table, he kept his hands firmly on my hips. His smile didn't disappear as he looked at me.

"What?"

"I don't know how to say this without you thinking I'm I some kind of pig, but that was fucking hot."

I shook my head, laughing. "You're welcome?"

A guy in a suit came over, leaning into Damon's ear. He nodded, then turned back to me.

"I have to go take care of something. I'll be right back." He pointed to where Grace and Giovanni were before leaving me to take care of business. "Try not to get into any fights while I'm gone, tough girl," he teased.

I danced over to Grace and Giovanni, feeling strangely invincible. When I filled them in on where Damon was, Giovanni went to join him in the back.

"Want to get a drink?" Grace asked. As I filled Grace in on what had happened, I heard a voice from the dance floor.

"Aww, he left you already for someone better, huh?"

I turned to see the same girl. She was becoming very annoying. Why couldn't she just leave me alone? My patience was wearing thin as she gave me a look of victory.

"Look out, your desperation is showing," I laughed.

When Grace and I turned to walk away, she shoved me. I paused, handing my drink to Grace.

"Hold this?"

I turned, shoving her back as hard as I could. She fell backward onto the floor. The other people around her moved to form a circle around us.

"Leave now, before you get hurt," I warned her.

She jumped to her feet, getting back in my face. She seemed relentless in her attempts to make me feel like a lesser person. But I wasn't, was I? My insides began to crack. Was I even worth Damon's time? She was wrong, right?

"Did he leave you because he realized you weren't good enough, or did he just get tired of your pathetic attempts to get with him?"

A single word rang inside me, as I had heard Austin say it a million times—*pathetic*. I was on the edge of a breakdown right there. How could one word affect me so much? She thought it too, obviously; it wasn't just Austin. Maybe they were right; maybe I was pathetic. I felt a hand on my shoulder.

"Come on, Noelle, she's nothing."

It was Grace, her voice like an angel, snatching me from my terrible thoughts. As I turned to walk away, the girl spun me back around, slapping my face. I looked at her, shocked for only a moment. Then something came over me and, without thinking, I punched her. She stumbled backward, looking to me, her hand to her mouth, her lip bleeding. A guy ran to her, and then looked my way. He was visibly angry as he charged closer to me. I covered my head, bracing for impact, like I had done a million times before. But before he could get within reach, Damon ran out from the back, stood in front of me, shielding me behind him.

"You better watch your friend," he told Damon. "She touches my girlfriend again and she'll pay for it," he snapped.

Damon took a step toward him, "Is that a threat?"

His voice was calm but dominant as he gave the guy a look. The guy swallowed hard as Giovanni walked over. He glanced from Damon to Giovanni.

"Fuck," he shouted. "You're the Amoretti brothers...aren't you?" He turned to his girlfriend. "What are you doing, starting drama with them? Are you trying to get me killed?" He turned back to Damon. "I'm sorry, man. I didn't know—"

Damon waved over a guy in a suit. "Escort this guy and his girlfriend out, please."

He nodded, grabbing the guy and his girlfriend by the arms. Damon turned to face me. I panicked, trying to think of what to say so he wouldn't be upset with me.

"Damon, it's my fault, I'm sorry. It won't happen again, I—"

He put his hands on my face. I searched his eyes for anger, holding my breath. But instead, he laughed.

"Can't stay out of trouble for five minutes, can you?" He shook his head, but there was a hint of a smile on his face. "You don't have to apologize. She put her hands on you, you defended yourself. I have to go in the back for another minute. Will you be fine out here?"

"Yeah, I think so, now that she's gone."

He laughed once more, shaking his head, before disappearing into the back. Grace and I sat at the bar, only waiting a moment before the bartender slid a shot toward me.

"From the guy in the blue T-shirt," she pointed. I could only see the back of his head.

"He also said to give you this." She handed me a note. I looked to Grace before taking it to read.

Meet me on the dance floor. Max

I jumped out of my seat. "I'll be back!" I informed Grace without hesitation.

I walked out onto the dance floor, making it to the middle. I felt arms around me, and I turned to see Max. He had a huge tattoo down his arm and was growing out a beard. His cheeks were sunken in. He was thin and he looked like he hadn't slept in weeks. But when he hugged me, it was him—my best friend.

"I miss you," I admitted.

He guided me to the other side of the club opposite the bar. He hugged me again.

"I miss you more," he smiled. "What are you doing here? Wait, who are you here with? Austin?"

"Well, I ended it with Austin, with a lot of help from Damon. That's who I'm here with, along with his brother, Giovanni, and his wife, Grace.

He smiled. "I'd hoped so. That's the best news I've heard since I got here!"

"What do you mean you hoped so?"

He swallowed, his smile dwindling.

"Max, what don't I know?"

"All right, I'm the one who sent you those pictures."

My brows furrowed. "But I have your number."

"Right, but I sent them from a burner." He sighed, "Look I got those pictures from a friend who saw him and knew I had a connection with you. I wasn't going to send them but I couldn't let you live with that cheating bastard anymore. You would be happier without him and I thought you just needed a little…push. I'm sorry for the hurt it caused you while you were going through it and I'm sorry I couldn't be there for you."

I reached up, putting my hand on his cheek.

"You *were* there for me Max. Thank you for always wanting to see me happy." I pulled him back in for another hug. "So, tell me, how's the job? Do you like it?" I asked.

"The job is all right, extremely different than what I was doing back in town. But I can't wait until I'm done. I really can't talk about it, but—listen, Noelle—" He paused, his eyes darting all around as he leaned in the speak close to my ear. "Be careful around Damon, okay? I'm going to be outside when you guys leave and whatever you hear me say, it's not going to be the nicest. Whatever you do, don't let on that you know me and please don't let them say my real name."

"I'm not even sure they would recognize you with all this ink and your facial hair—I barely recognize you, Max."

He quickly brought his finger to his lips. "Shh, Noelle."

"Sorry," I whispered.

"If anyone says my real name, it could blow my cover."

"Okay, I understand. I won't let them."

He rested his forehead against mine. My emotions had been all over the place, but in that moment, I felt at peace. I peeked back to Grace. She was trying to look preoccupied, but I could tell she was watching me. When Damon and Giovanni came out of the back, I knew I had to get back before one of them saw me.

"I have to go. Damon is going to look for me."

He smiled, "I know."

He kissed my cheek, hugging me for another moment before disappearing into the crowd. I walked back to the group. Grace gave me a look of confusion before standing up.

"Ready to get going?" Damon asked.

I nodded as the guys led the way. Grace pulled me back to walk with her.

"Who was that?" she asked.

"An old friend."

I knew she wanted more information, but that was all I was willing to give. We walked outside to see three guys leaning on their cars—one of them, Max. Grace shot me an immediate, even more confused look. I reached out, taking hold of Damon's arm.

"I knew these were your Lamborghinis...leave it to the Amoretti boys to drive the flashiest cars in town," one taunted. "I thought you two were gone...was I misinformed?"

"Absolutely. Now get the fuck off my car," Damon ordered.

His tone was dark and demanding. I could tell he was looking at Max, trying to figure out how he knew him.

"I see you added another one to your group. What's your name, beautiful?" the guy asked me.

Damon pulled me behind him. "Leave now, before someone gets hurt."

"Our boss wants to know why you two are back in town," he said, turning toward Giovanni.

"We're here because we own this club. Just because we don't live here doesn't mean the city's up for grabs," Giovanni shot back.

"If your boss has an issue with that, he can let us know...not the lowest fucking men on the totem pole."

"Yeah, I'm sure he'll be happy to hear that," Max spat back, each word laced with sarcasm.

"Good," Damon took another step toward them. "Now fucking leave." They did as he said, pausing to give me another look.

On the way home, I must have fallen asleep. The sound of Damon's garage door closing woke me up. As we walked inside, Grace came charging through the front door. She looked angry. Giovanni ran after her, shouting something in Italian to Damon. Whatever he said, he was too late. Grace had made it to me, stopping just a foot away from me.

"Who is he?" she yelled.

Damon got between us. "What the hell, Grace?"

Giovanni kept her close as she continued to yell at me.

"I saw her with one of those guys from Montero's crew. He kissed her on the cheek in the club just before we left. She was hugging him."

Damon's eyebrows pulled together, shaking his head slightly as he glanced back to me. He stepped back so that he could get a view of everyone.

"How do you know she isn't just here for information about us?" she continued. "The only explanation I can come up with is that she is working for him. Think about it—Austin works for Montero. What if she's just trying to gain information for him? What if this all has been a big setup?"

"Why would I do that?" I tried to defend myself. "I don't even know who Montero is!"

"Why were you talking to that guy?" Grace demanded, crossing her arms. "You said he was an old friend."

"Because he *is* an old friend," I yelled out, unable to stop myself.

Everyone stopped talking. Damon finally turned toward me. His eyes squinted at me, then widened.

"Noelle, was that…Max?"

I didn't answer, I couldn't. If I gave him up, what kind of friend would I be?

"I have to go," I tried escaping only for Damon to take my hand in his.

He guided me back to him. "It's okay, you don't have to say it. I thought I recognized him anyway. We're not going to blow his cover, don't worry. It's good to know what he's up to, though. Then we can make sure he doesn't get caught in the crossfire."

"He's a cop, undercover in Montero's organization," Giovanni relayed to the others. "Now let us calm down, all right?" His phone chimed before anyone spoke another word. I could tell by the way his shoulders tensed up, his eyes meeting Damon's before returning to his phone, it wasn't good news.

Chapter **Twelve**

"WE HAVE TO GO BACK TO THE CITY," HE SAID. "FIVE minutes."

They started speaking in Italian, Giovanni filling Damon in on what was going on. It was eleven o'clock, what could possibly be happening?

"I'll go get the car and meet you outside in a few minutes. Grace, you want to stay here with Noelle or head home?"

"I'll stay."

He nodded, giving her a kiss and telling her he loved her before heading out the front door.

"I'll be back in a couple of hours," said Damon.

"Be careful."

I watched as he grabbed a gun from the front closet. He loaded it, clicking it back like he could do it with his eyes closed. He tucked it behind him, covering it with his black T-shirt. A car horn sounded out front.

"I'll be back, don't worry." He half-smiled. He was gone seconds later.

"Come on, I like to put on a comedy when they have to go to work like this." She gestured for me to follow behind her to the living room. "It helps take my mind off of it."

"Does this happen often?"

"Not too often, but when it does it always makes me nervous." She turned on the first one that popped up on Damon's giant television.

I took a blanket from the back of the couch, hugging it to myself for comfort. My heart was beating a million times a minute. They would be okay, right? Of course, they would, they do this for a living. Whatever *this* was.

"Grace," I started, getting her attention, "I-I'm sorry."

"For what?"

"For making you think that I had some kind of ulterior motive. I would never do anything to hurt any of you and I want you to know that. I will be forever grateful for everything you've done for me because I wouldn't be here if it weren't for you three."

She let out a quiet sigh.

"I knew that deep down, but when I saw that same guy outside, I went into protect-the-family mode. I wish you would have just told me who he was."

"I couldn't betray him. He told me it was undercover and I wasn't allowed to tell anyone. It was for his safety." I looked down at my hands. "Now that you know though I guess it'll be easier for me to talk about it."

"What is he doing? What's his job?"

"That, I don't know. I didn't even know he was a part of Montero's crew until tonight. I didn't expect to see him at all until the job was done."

"Montero's already in jail. I'm not sure what their angle is unless they are going after his son who's running their organization now through his father's orders." She thought out loud before shrugging, "either way I understand your need to protect him, but I want you to understand my need to protect my family as well."

"I do."

"Good, because you are one heck of a girlfriend." She hugged me.

My body relaxed at her gesture, wrapping my arms around her to give her a squeeze. I curled back up onto the couch, looking up at the movie playing. It wasn't long before I fell asleep right where I was.

I felt someone carrying me. I jumped awake, grabbing onto whatever I could.

"It's me," he whispered softly. I opened my eyes as Damon set me down on a bed.

"What time is it?"

"Two in the morning. I didn't mean to wake you. Do you want me to take you home?"

"No, it's okay." I pulled back the covers, curling up into bed. He covered me up.

"My room is down the hall to the right, if you need anything."

I smiled. "Thanks." I heard him turn on the shower before falling back to sleep.

That next morning, I woke up as sunlight crept through the window. I stretched, sitting up. The house was quiet when I walked out into the hallway. Damon's door was open. I peeked in, not seeing him. His bed was made up perfectly. I fought the urge to be nosy, and instead turned to walk downstairs. Hearing strange noises from the basement, I went to investigate. There were weights and workout equipment on one side and an open area on the other. The room was covered with mats from floor to ceiling. I watched, surprised, as Damon and Grace sparred, Grace dodging and returning punches, while Giovanni sat, watching. I wished I could do that, but with all the time spent with Austin, I felt like a completely different woman than I once was. I knew if I tried to fight like that I might cower under the guy swinging at me. Maybe not if it was a woman, but definitely a man would send me over the edge. Maybe it was just too soon. They took a break when they noticed I was watching.

"Hey, Noelle!" Damon smiled as sweat dripped down his forehead.

Grace walked over to me as Giovanni and Damon started to fight.

We watched in silence, as the guys sparred.

"You guys ready for a run?" Giovanni asked, wiping his face with a towel.

"I'll have to make a stop at my apartment to change," I pointed out.

As we got closer to the store, something in my gut began to twist. As we got closer to the building, I realized why, taking off in a full sprint. There was a fire truck out front, firefighters milling about. I paused for only a moment as my heart sank. The entire building was burned, one side of it caved in. The backside brick of the building was still standing. I ran to one of the firemen standing to the side.

"What happened?"

"Ms. Taylor, I'm sorry. I know you just reopened recently. The cause of the fire is under investigation and we are going to do everything we can to help."

"What do you mean 'under investigation'?"

"It seems that the fire started from the ground floor. The front window was smashed from the outside. We are still collecting evidence. I will keep you updated as we progress. I'm sure Officer Wells will want to speak with you at some point."

I knew who was responsible for it; there was no need for investigation. Austin. He was the one behind this. I ran toward the back door. Damon called after me as I threw the door open, carelessly running inside. Everything in the back of the store was soaked from the fire hoses. I picked up a book from the floor, flipping through the burned, sopping wet pages. I heard them calling me from outside. I trudged back through the rubble, making my way outside. No words came out, as I couldn't take my eyes off the crumbling building I had called my home. What looked like spray paint on the corner of the building caused me to take a closer look. There on the side of the building, half burned away, were the words, *Now You Have Nothing.*

Anger began to grow inside me. Why was I so stupid to think that I could leave him? I ran my hands through my hair, crying angry tears.

"Noelle, I'm so sorry—" Grace began, putting her hand on my shoulder.

I shrugged her off. "This is all your fault!" I yelled at them. "If you would have just left me alone like I asked, this wouldn't have happened!"

"We can help you," she offered.

"I think you have done enough," I responded. "I made a mistake letting you in. Just stay away from me!"

Damon reached out for me, his face showing how hurt he was. I took a step away.

"I don't want to see you anymore." I turned, running away.

Not knowing exactly where to go, I ended up at Max's house. I sat on his front porch, putting my head on my knees. Why did I leave Austin when I knew this was going to happen? I knew I shouldn't have told them anything. I had nothing now, nowhere to go. If I went back to Damon's, it would only cause Austin to antagonize me more instead of leaving me alone. That is, unless...I went back to Austin's. Would he even let me stay after everything? He would forgive me, right? I was so stupid to leave him, he was right. My growing self-loathing wouldn't let me sit there any longer. I sprinted around the small town, running down every single road. I stopped when I reached the bar. I rested my body against the side of the building. I was panting to catch my breath when I felt the hairs on the back of my neck stand on end.

"Do you need somewhere to stay tonight?"

I looked up to see Austin standing in front of me. Unable to form words, I nodded.

"Come on, you can take a shower and get cleaned up," he whispered running the backs of his fingers lightly down my cheek.

I walked beside him, down the sidewalk. We didn't get far when a car skidded to a stop beside us. Damon and Giovanni jumped out.

"Noelle? What are you doing?" Damon asked in disbelief.

"She's coming home, where she belongs," Austin answered for me.

"The fuck she is," he snapped. "Noelle, think about what you are going back to."

"Damon, go away," I ordered through tears.

Silence fell between all four of us before he shook his head.

"No fucking way." He walked toward me, using one finger to tilt my chin up to face him.

When Austin tried to get between Damon and I, Giovanni shoved him away.

"Think about the hell you lived in with him. Is that what you are choosing to return to?"

No matter how much I hated to admit it, he was right. I didn't want to go back with Austin. Who knows what he would do to me once we were alone, but how could I go with Damon knowing it would egg Austin on?

"I will go with you now, but only until I clear my head. Then I will figure out where I'm going."

"Okay," Damon agreed, immediately. "That's fine."

He opened the car door for me, hearing Austin growl as I moved to get in.

"Think about this Noelle. There are consequences to every action."

"Shut the fuck up, asshole." Giovanni snapped, tossing him down so hard this time he fell backward onto the ground.

I looked down at my hands; all I wanted in this moment was to just be alone and safe. The only place for the safe part, was Damon's. I could figure out a way to be alone once I got there. I sat down in the back seat of the car. Damon climbed in next to me. Giovanni got in the front seat, speeding away. I pushed Damon away as he reached out to stroke my hair, trying to calm me down. Well, I was sick of being calm.

"Don't be mad at me," Damon said. "Please."

"Why couldn't you just leave me alone?" I finally belted out.

"Noelle, he beat you. I'm not letting you go back to that."

"This is all your fault, why can't you just go away?" I sobbed. "Before you came into my life, I could handle it, and now—now everything has completely blown up!"

He put his hands on my face so I would look at him. "He cheated on you, he *raped* you, and he tried to kill you!" he yelled. "I don't care if you hate me the rest of your life, I'm not letting you go back there."

I scooted away from him, pulling my knees to my chest. I sat silently crying until we got to his house. He stepped out of the car, pulling me to my feet. I marched into the house, making a beeline for the stairs.

"Noelle, wait."

"Why? Why can't you leave me alone?" I snapped at him from midway up the stairs.

"I will if that is what you want, but only when I know you are safe from that asshole. What were you thinking going back home with him?"

"I was thinking about how stupid I was to believe that I could just run away from him and be happy. I will never be happy because of him, but at least I could have had my store with him. At least I could have kept all the things that money can't buy. The only things I had left from my parents were in that store and now they are gone. And it's my fault for trusting you. I shouldn't have told you anything and just went home that night."

"Home to what? Getting hit by that asshole?" he snapped, "I'm sorry for what he did to you, but can't you see you are safe now?"

"I'm safe? I was supposed to be in that apartment this morning. If I wouldn't have stayed here, I'd be gone, Damon. He doesn't care; he's just going to keep coming at me until he wins. Me going back to him is a version of him winning, don't you see? It's survival. I don't understand why you think anything otherwise."

I was exhausted and devastated. I wanted to go to sleep and wake up to this being all just one big nightmare. My store would be there and my parents' things would still be there. I walked up the rest of the stairs.

"I'll stay here for tonight and then I'm leaving. When I do, you are going to leave me alone."

I didn't know where I would go, maybe Max's or maybe even

back to Austin. If I went back to him maybe I could clean out the store and still have the piece of land. I could rebuild and try to save anything that wasn't completely destroyed by the fire, if there was anything left.

I slammed the bedroom door behind me. Curling up on the bed, I cried myself to sleep.

I woke up with a blanket over me. I heard Damon talking in the hallway. It sounded like he was getting closer. The door opened slowly as he walked inside. He sat a shopping bag down at the end of the bed before turning to me.

"Grace brought you these to start replacing what you had."

I turned away from him, still angry. I heard him sigh behind me.

"There are towels in the bathroom closet, if you want to get a shower."

The door clicked shut behind him. The longer I lay there, the more enticing a hot shower sounded. I let out a growl as I threw myself off the bed. I started the shower, digging through the bag of clothes Damon brought in. Thirty minutes later, I was still in the shower, letting the hot water beat down on my back. A knock at the bathroom door made me scream.

"Sorry! I was coming to check on you, you've been in there a while," Grace said.

"I'm fine," I responded, shutting the water off.

Once dressed, I came downstairs. Damon was eating a sandwich as I walked into the kitchen.

"Do you want something to eat?" he asked.

"No."

I turned around, leaving the room. My stomach felt like a rock. I was emotionally exhausted and didn't know what to feel. I was devastated and needed someone to blame for it. I walked into the library, only to have him follow me.

"Let me make you something to eat," he offered.

"I don't want to see you, go away," I snapped.

"Well, that's going to be hard since you are staying here," he snapped back.

"Oh, yeah, maybe I'll just go home. Oh wait, I don't have a home anymore, thanks to you."

"How is it *my* fault?" he yelled. "I didn't burn it down, he did. Why are you blaming me?" I flinched as he threw his hands into the air. He noticed, and took a step back, saying softly now, "I'm sorry. But—"

"If you would have just left me alone, none of this would have happened," I interrupted.

"If I would have left you alone, he would have killed you or you would have killed yourself. Either way, you would be dead, Noelle."

"Maybe it would be better that way," I spat. "What do I have left? Nothing. No family, no store…" I paused, lowering my voice before continuing. "No purpose."

In my attempt to walk past him he pulled me back into the library, shutting the doors behind him. He sat me down on the couch, knocking a book out of the way. Kneeling to look into my eyes, his expression turned soft.

"Don't talk like that. You may have lost your store, but not your purpose. There is a reason you weren't in your apartment last night. You are alive for a reason. Don't ever think you have lost purpose." He sighed a desperate sigh. "What about Max? You have him. You have me, and Giovanni, and Grace, all here to help you."

"I don't need help, I just want you to leave me alone," I said.

"Well, too bad, because I'm going to be here to help you get through this, whether you like it or not."

I stood up, walking back upstairs. I locked the bedroom door behind me so he couldn't come in again. Lying on the bed, all I could think about was the store.

All those nights of helping my mom stock while my dad did the same. He'd take her hand and dance up and down the aisles. She'd pretend to hate it, but her smile betrayed her, showing just how much she enjoyed every moment of it. Then I'd pout until he'd do the same with me.

The nights where he worked on cases as I got older in the back room. I'd go back there with my homework, pretending it was a case of my own. When I finished, he'd talk to me about laws that pertained to the case. Through high school we'd work on cases together upstairs in the apartment where the specifics of the cases wouldn't be overheard by customers shopping for books.

That store held a lot of memories, all ones that warmed me from within. Those memories would have to live in my mind now, they wouldn't surround me while I was in the walls of the store or living in the apartment above. That part of them was gone. I became so depressed, I couldn't move. I never got up or even changed position on the bed.

Damon knocked on the door as the sun went down. I ignored

him as he knocked a second time. "Noelle?" His voice was muffled from the other side of the door. "At least let me know you are alive."

"Yeah," I said, just loudly enough for him to hear me.

"Can you eat something, please? You haven't eaten anything all day."

I ignored him, wishing he would just leave me alone to sink deeper into my thoughts. I was almost asleep when he knocked again. When I didn't answer him, he tried to open the door.

"Noelle, unlock the door. I don't want it locked after what you said earlier."

I smashed my eyes shut, and covered my ears with my pillow. I wanted him to go away. I wanted the *world* to just go away.

"Noelle?"

The longer I refused to say anything, the more he started to panic. I heard him run down the stairs, then back up. The handle of the door wiggled for a moment before he walked in. The keys still jingled in the door lock as he ran to me. I looked at him, still speaking no words. As he raised his hand to run his fingers through his hair, I flinched, pulling my arms over my head. He froze, slowly lowering his arm back to his side. The next thing I felt was a soft touch to my arms. He sat down on the edge of the bed.

"I would never lay a hand on you," he whispered.

Tears were now beginning to fall from my eyes.

"I just want to be happy, Damon," I cried, sitting up. "I just want to belong somewhere again."

He wrapped his strong arms around me. His touch helped calm me as I closed my eyes, head on his shoulder.

"You will. Just get through this, and let me help you."

I nodded into his shoulder.

"Come eat something, please. I'll go get you anything you want if you don't want to eat what I made."

I really didn't have an appetite, but I followed him into the kitchen. The air smelled sweet, a scent that my nose welcomed but couldn't place. He got out a plate and handed me a spoon. I looked at the dish he'd set out. It was filled with white balls that looked like dumplings. I heard him chuckle.

"It's gnocchi, a potato dumpling. I also made tortellini to go with it, which are noodles stuffed with meat and cheese."

"You made this?"

"Yeah...but if you don't like it, that's okay, we can order you something—anything you want."

I scooped up a gnocchi, spooning it into my mouth. It was delicious and I glanced at him.

"YOU made this?"

"I did." He smiled. "Don't sound so surprised, there's more to me that just a pretty face, you know."

I put more on my plate, doing the same with the pasta. The more I ate, the more I started to feel something coming to life within me. As I finished eating, he started to do the dishes.

"Can I help?" I muttered.

"If you want. You don't have to, though."

I needed something to do, anything. I stood beside him, drying the dishes as he handed them to me. Since I had no idea where anything went, I watched as he put them away.

"Want to play a video game or something?" he asked hopefully, scratching the back of his head.

"Sure."

His smile showed his relief I wasn't going back upstairs. He hurried me into the living room, probably assuming I'd change my mind. Turning on the game system, he handed me a controller. I sat down in front of him on the floor. After many failed attempts at playing, I put the controller down.

"I don't get it, I can't do it," I sighed.

He paused the game and gave me a run down on the buttons. As I practiced playing with his guidance, he put his hands on my shoulders while he told me what buttons to push. I actually was playing better. He squeezed my shoulders, then rubbed the back of my neck with his thumbs. I began to focus more on what his hands were doing than the game I was playing. I leaned back, looking up at him.

"You know it's hard to concentrate with you rubbing my neck like that."

He held his hands up. "Sorry."

His smile was innocent, like he didn't even realize he was doing it. I smiled to myself as I turned my attention back to the game. Silence fell over us for only a moment before police lights reflected through the front window. I looked to Damon, confused as two officers began making their way to the door. As we got up, I noticed two officers walking to Giovanni's door, too. Whatever was going on didn't look good.

Chapter **Thirteen**

DAMON CAUTIOUSLY OPENED THE DOOR TO SEE TWO officers standing there. When they saw me, they barged right in, pushing him against the wall, quickly putting him in handcuffs. I stood there, confused. Did they have a warrant? They couldn't just come in without permission or a warrant and arrest him like that. What were they even arresting him for? An officer looked at me, pulling his radio toward his mouth.

"I got her, she's safe," he spoke into his radio, then turned to me. "It's going to be okay, you're safe now."

"What?" I asked, confused. "I was never in danger, what do you mean?"

"Noelle, we have evidence you were abducted by Damon and Giovanni Amoretti."

"Abducted, no, you're confused." I looked to Damon.

The officer slammed him against the wall. "Thought you were invincible, didn't you Mr. Amoretti?"

I tried to grab the officer to pull him away from Damon. "Stop, he didn't do anything!"

They began walking him to the squad cars outside. I followed closely behind to see Giovanni in the same situation. Before they got into the cars, I stopped the officer again.

"Wait, I am an adult, you can't arrest them. It was my decision to go with them."

"True, but we can still get them for false imprisonment," he smiled.

"No, you can't. I chose to come here and I could have left at any time. I've stayed here before. Whoever gave you this information is wrong."

"We have a witness that stated he saw Damon Amoretti carrying you over his shoulder and throwing you in his car to which Giovanni Amoretti was driving. How do you explain that?"

"He did no such thing! Since I am an adult and was not being held against my will, you have to let them go. Without any testimony against them, you have no case." I was panicking, trying to think of anything that would help get them released.

He looked at the other officers. "I think she may have Stockholm syndrome."

I crossed my arms. "Not possible. I *chose* to stay here, plus that takes a long time to set in unless it's a life-or-death situation. Which, as I explained once already, I am perfectly safe here."

He opened his mouth to protest again. I cut him off, tired of Austin and his attempts to ruin everything for me.

"Let them go or I will come after you for wrongful arrest." I took a step closer to him. "Think about your case right now, you have nothing but a 'witness' that also doubles as my crazy ex-boy-friend," I paused, trying to read his face. "Do you not remember who my father was?"

All of them were speechless. I didn't back down, just stared at him until he gave the order to let Giovanni and Damon go. The officer looked at them. "I'll be watching you," he said climbing in his car and speeding away. Once they were gone, I broke down, feeling horrible for what had happened.

"I'm sorry, this is my fault," I cried. "You guys don't deserve this. This is my problem and you two almost got arrested because of me." I walked back into the house.

I made my way back to the room I was staying in. I felt over-come by guilt. All of this chaos was coming from me and I was only making life worse for them. I stared out the window into the back yard. The sun was going down, making the woods behind Damon's house seem eerie. I didn't move as I heard the door open, Damon stepping inside. He said nothing, just pulled me close. I leaned into him, feeling the tears coming again. His arms tight-ened around me. I let him hold me, feeling him run his fingers softly through my hair. It gave me the most euphoric feeling, like I was floating on a cloud without a care in the world. We lay down on the bed together, facing one another. He ran the fingertips up the side of my arm and back down leaving a trail of goosebumps in their wake. My body was overcome with the need to be closer to him. I wanted this peaceful feeling he brought me to last, to drown in the comfort he'd gifted me with. What would happen if I moved closer? Would he expect something? I peeked up at him through my lashes.

"Damon?" I whispered.

"Hmm?"

"Can I be in this moment with you?"

His brows pulled together. "Aren't you already?"

"Kind of." I sighed, "My brain is trained on thinking three steps ahead. I go through every decision I make just to figure out what consequences could come of each choice. It doesn't stop. There have even been nights I can't get to sleep because my brain is already going through what was to come the next morning. I just want to be present with you...completely in the moment without having to strategize about the possible outcomes." I paused, pulling my lower lip between my teeth.

"Keep going."

"Can I-"" I had no idea how to phrase it to tell him exactly what I needed, but I tried because I felt in my heart that he was the one that could give it to me. "Can I do something reckless and carefree to just *be* in this moment with you without having consequences or it leading to anything else?" I rambled.

He nodded his head slightly. His tongue subconsciously wetting his lips before he swallowed. I propped myself up onto my elbow, my eyes dipping down from his eyes to his lips. My heart was beating frantically in my chest like a hummingbird's wings. He didn't move, instead I moved to him. I kissed him fearlessly without my brain formulating a plan as to what would happen next. I leaned into him. He kissed me back, tucking his fingers gently into my hair at the back of my head. His hands never explored my body as I climbed on top of him. They stayed tangled with my hair, caressing my head. Finally, I pulled back breathless and lips numb, examining his expression. I felt my cheeks heat up, knowing they were red.

"I-uh-" I tried to begin explaining, "I'm, I-"

He shook his head, tucking a strand of hair behind my ear.

"It's okay, I understand," he whispered, his breath a shadow of a lingering kiss against my lips. "It doesn't have to be more than this moment."

I nodded, collapsing slowly onto him. My cheek pressed against his chest as my heart filled with joy. He understood. He got it--got *me*. The steady rise and fall of his chest made it feel as though I was being rocked to sleep. Just as my droopy eyes began to close, he whispered into my hair.

"We are going to get through this together."

I slept through most of the night, only waking up once when I felt an arm reach around me. My first reaction was to panic—Austin would reach around me the same way. This woke Damon as he moved his arm away.

"You okay?" he said softly into my ear. "Is that all right?"

"Yeah," was all I could manage before he inched closer, falling right back to sleep.

The next morning, he was gone when I woke up. I felt better than I had the day before. Grace was downstairs with the guys as I peeked into the kitchen. They greeted me with smiles.

"We're going to my parents' for a little bit, are you up to coming along?" Damon asked nervously, scratching the back of his head.

Before I could respond Grace grabbed my hand. "You should come," she said with a smile.

"I'll go throw some fresh clothes on," I mumbled, looking down at the clothes I was in the day before.

We only had a two-minute walk to Damon's parents' house. Damon kept close as we approached the front door. I began to get butterflies in my stomach as I thought about meeting his parents. Although I was unsure why I felt this way. I mean, we weren't dating or anything. As I stepped inside, I heard the pleasant sound of a familiar voice. I stood up straight, following the sound of the voice quietly. Walking down a short hallway, I began to peek into a doorway that was cracked open.

"Noelle, you can't go in there," Damon whispered. "That's my father's office."

I looked back to Damon, then through the space between the door and frame. That voice was so familiar! Damon reached out to stop me but it was too late. I stepped right into the room, almost like I had done it a million times before. The man I was assuming was Damon's father had his back to me, on the phone. Damon cleared his throat, causing his father to turn around.

"Stefano!" I shouted, running toward him as his face came into view.

He quickly hung up the phone and reached out to hug me.

"Noelle? What are you doing here?"

By the time Damon could process anything, Giovanni and Grace were standing behind him.

"What is going on?" Giovanni asked. "How do you two know each other?"

"I've known Noelle since she was a child," Stefano explained. "Her father was one of my best friends." He paused, looking to Damon. "I should have figured it was *this* Noelle you were referring to when we spoke, I have not run into any other 'Noelles' in my life."

I crossed my arms. "What did you tell him about me?"

Damon laughed nervously. "Nothing, really. I just told him about Austin so I could use some of his resources…that's all."

Stefano looked to me. "Anything you need, Noelle, you tell me, and it's done."

I thanked him, feeling a bit weird that Damon was Stefano's son. It was brought up that he had children only every time my father and he got together. They would always ask about one another's family. When I would listen in, I'd hear what great things they were accomplishing in the city. I'd never met them. Most of the time when I saw Stefano, it was when he came to visit my father.

"This is such a coincidence, Noelle! I tried to call you yesterday but it said your number was out of service," he explained. "I wanted to meet up with you. Do you have time now?" he asked.

"Yeah. I mean, I think this was the plan today."

"Great." He turned toward the guys and Grace. "Give us the room," he ordered.

Giovanni and Grace turned to leave without hesitation. Damon was a different story. He stood there for a moment before saying something in Italian to his father. A chuckle from Stefano escaped as he answered Damon's question. Damon then shut the door behind him, leaving us alone.

"Please, sit," Stefano pointed to the chair next to the one he sat in. "I may have come across some information about your parents' death and have a couple questions, if you are up for it."

I nodded. I was up for anything that would help solve their murder.

"Take me through the night you got the news."

"I was out at the clearing with Max and some friends. I got home around nine and got ready for bed. I was watching television in the living room when I got the call."

"And what did you do after that?"

"I called Max to tell him what happened. He came over after that. Then I called Austin and did the same. He was working, but he left work early to come home. They both stayed with me that night."

"Did anything seem out of place or weird at their funeral to you?"

I thought back. "Not that I can remember, but I clung to Austin the whole time. I wasn't really looking at the people who came. I remember feeling numb over it all."

He got up, heading toward the door. "If you remember anything, let me know immediately. Let's join the others, shall we?"

As I followed him to the kitchen, I realized I had already met Damon and Giovanni's mom once. She must have remembered me, because she hugged me as I came through the doorway. It gave me a small bit of peace as I reminisced with Stefano, the others listening in, asking questions to clear things up they didn't understand. We sat there all afternoon. Before I knew it, it was time to head back to Damon's. We ended up sitting out back on his patio.

"Okay, so your fathers were friends, I get that, but how did you not know Damon before you met him at the bar?" Grace asked.

"Stefano never brought anyone with him when he came to meet with my dad except for a couple guys." I turned to Damon. "Remember when I told you I used to sit outside my dad's office and listen to him speak Italian to his friend from the city?"

"Yeah."

"Your dad is that friend. I met your mom once; she came with him for dinner but that was it."

"But didn't you connect his last name with ours?" Giovanni asked.

"I didn't know his last name. He was always just Stefano."

"That's kind of nice that you know their parents already," Grace said.

"You mean kind of weird that they are connected?" Giovanni laughed.

The corners of Damon's lips turned up into a small smile. "It is very weird how they are connected," he agreed.

As nightfall started to come, Grace and Giovanni stood.

"Are you guys up for a movie?" Damon smiled.

"No," responded Giovanni. "I think we're going to call it a night."

Damon turned to me as we got inside. "How about you?"

"Yeah, why not?" I half smiled, still high on how relaxing it was to catch up with Stefano that day.

I followed him downstairs to a room with three couches and

a giant screen on the wall. I sat down as he set everything up. As the movie trailers began, I turned to Damon.

"Thanks, by the way."

His expression was somewhat confused. "For what?"

"Staying with me last night." I paused. "I haven't slept that well in a long time and—" I looked down at my hands as I felt my face get flushed. "I felt safe with you there, it was nice."

I saw him smile out of the corner of my eye.

"You know, if you want you can sleep in my room with me..." his smile widened. "With or without clothes, totally up to you."

I laughed, rolling my eyes. "You do know how to create a moment, don't you?"

"I try," he said as he laughed.

I turned back to the movie, getting comfy in my spot. About halfway through, Damon put his arm on the back of the couch. Without saying a word, I inched closer, resting my side against him. As his hand slid onto my arm, he leaned forward.

"You are cold as ice." He stood up, grabbing a blanket from the closet. "Why didn't you say anything?"

Curling up in the blanket next to him I shrugged my shoulder. "I'm not that cold."

As he put his arm back around my shoulders, I looked up toward him. His eyes locked on mine. I froze, feeling nervous. It overpowered my body so much I started to giggle, looking away for only a second before returning my gaze to his eyes. He put his hand on my cheek so gently it gave me goose bumps. He pressed his lips softly against mine. I felt my entire body melt in that moment.

Every worry I had flew out the window, as the only thing I could think about was how happy I was. He pulled his lips away from mine, but only for a second.

"Holy shit," he whispered, smiling, coming in for another kiss.

This time, inner panic set in. All I could think of were the things Austin said to me. This made me question myself, in what should have been a beautiful moment. *Why me? I'm not worth anything, so why? I'm sure I'm not what he really wants. I'm broken and not worth any of his time. He could do so much better than me.* Or did he just want a physical relationship. Would he take it whenever he wanted it? It was overwhelming to think about getting that close to someone again. I quickly pushed away from him as tears stung my eyes.

"I—I have t—to go." I tripped over my words as I ran toward the stairs.

Damon called after me, begging me to stop, but I couldn't. I wanted to get as far away from him as possible. This was not what he really wanted; I knew that for a fact. I was a waste of his time. He should be out there chasing the woman who was going to make him happy...the one that would be his *one*...not me. I ran out the front door and straight to the waterfall. I knew Damon would know where I was going, but I hoped he didn't come looking for me. I wasn't worthy of any more of his time, especially when I knew he didn't really want someone so broken.

Chapter **Fourteen**

I WAS SITTING NEXT TO THE WATERFALL, FEET DANGLING off the edge, when I heard a rustling in the trees. I assumed it was Damon coming for an explanation. I didn't want to face him just yet, so I continued to stare out at the water below me. When I finally looked up, I saw Grace taking a spot next to me.

Before I had a chance to say anything, she held up a finger. "I brought some wine."

A reassuring smile spread slowly across her face as she held the bottle out to me. Pausing for only a second, I took the bottle and began opening it. She dug around in her bag, pulling out two wine glasses. At that point, I couldn't help but laugh.

"What?" she asked, smiling. "I figured we would be out here for a bit, sorting through why the hell Damon came barging through my front door like his ass was on fire."

I didn't say anything as she filled each glass, handing me one half full. She let me sit there for a few minutes until I felt ready to speak.

"I kissed him last night." I stated.

She took a sip of her wine, then gave me a nod to continue.

"I felt safe and we both understood that nothing was going to come from that. It was just for me to be in the moment without worrying about what would happen after."

"So, what happened tonight?"

"He kissed me," I began, taking a sip of wine. "He kissed me and...and at first I felt so happy, but then—" I stopped, not wanting to admit out loud all those other thoughts that flashed through my mind.

"Noelle, he likes you, a lot," she said with a half-smile. "You should see the look on his face when you walk into the room. I'm sure you don't even notice, but it happens every time."

"Yes, but he is just confused, Grace. Honestly, I am not worth his time. I'm pathetic and—"

"Stop!" she said firmly. "That is not true! I'll bet that's Austin talking. Damon likes you for who you are, no matter what." She paused. "I know that everything you went through was tougher than I could ever imagine, but you must know deep down, Austin's words are not the truth," Grace continued. "They are words he only says to manipulate you enough to think you have no one else to turn to. He wants complete control over you and that is how he gets it. Now that he isn't your boyfriend you have to take your life back. I know there is a firecracker of a woman in there, you just have to let her back out."

She wrapped me up in a hug, saying nothing more.

"I know what you are saying, I just...I don't want Damon to make a mistake." I paused once more, attempting to put together why he would want me. "Maybe he got these feelings because I'm staying with him. Maybe I'm too close, and because of that he caught feelings for me."

"Caught feelings? That's not possible," Grace smirked.

"Why not?"

She looked out at the water below. "Do you remember the first time you met them?"

I nodded. "Yeah, I served them at the bar."

"That night when they got home, all Damon could talk about was you. He went on for hours about how feisty and beautiful you were. He mentioned how you didn't even bat an eye before telling him like it was. He was impressed you knew the quote you three have tattooed on your bodies. For the first time in his life he met someone who couldn't care less about who he was. For the first time, he didn't meet a woman who was ready to marry him on the spot because of his name." She smiled. "You should have heard him begging Giovanni to go back to the bar with him just to see you again."

A short laugh escaped as I took another sip of my wine.

"I'm serious," she said. "My point is, he has liked you since the first time he met you. This is not because you are staying with him or that you are too close or that he's caught up in the whole rescue the damsel in distress thing—that's just not him, believe me."

I refilled my glass once more before taking a deep breath. "Well, what do I do now? I don't even know what to say to him."

"You tell him the truth."

We sat there in silence from then on. She stood up as we finished our wine. I did the same, following her closely as we walked back to Damon's house. At the front door, I paused to look at Grace. She gave me a nod and a wink. I stepped through the front door with my nerves on high alert.

"Damon is in the library. Grace and I are going out back if you need us for anything," Giovanni said, smiling encouragingly.

As I watched them disappear through the dining room, I looked toward the closed library doors. I took a deep breath, finally realizing that talking to Damon was something I *had* to do. Damon froze when he saw me enter the room. He took a few quick steps toward me before stopping.

"Noelle I—I am so sorry," he said, barely whispering. His face was tense, his hair now a disheveled mess on top of his head like he'd ran his fingers through it carelessly a million times.

My heart sank as I felt tears welling up in my eyes. I knew it. He was going to tell me it was a mistake, not anything else. He didn't mean for it to happen. It was exactly as I thought. Now I just had to stay quiet and listen.

"I didn't mean to scare you away or come on too strong. I had hoped you felt the same way I did. I just—I like you a lot and if you don't feel the same way, then that's okay. It won't happen again." He paused as a tear trickled down my cheek. "Wh—why are you crying?"

"You—you do like me?" was all I could muster. His face softened, his head tilting slightly to the side. I watched as his brows pulled together as if what I'd said puzzled him.

"Yes, so much, Noelle! Since that night at the bar when you busted me out about my tattoo," he laughed. "I knew then there was something about you I just couldn't shake. I thought about you all the time."

"I thought—I'm not whole, Damon. I don't feel like I am worthy enough to—"

"Stop," he interrupted. "You don't have to make excuses to push me away. If you don't like me, then just say so. It's okay, I'm a big boy, I can take it. But I don't want to hear any of the bullshit Austin told you, because that's exactly what it is, bullshit."

"I do like you," I blurted out. "I just don't know if you're sure, or—or if I'm ready to jump right back into a serious relationship."

He took a step closer, hesitantly putting his hands on my waist.

"I am one-hundred percent sure, and we don't have to rush into serious, Noelle. We can take this as slow as you want, *if* it's something you want. Either way, you are worth it to me, you mean a lot to me."

I took a deep breath, "Okay."

As he wrapped his strong arms around me, I got an overwhelming feeling of happiness. I started laughing a little, looking up at Damon.

"I'm sorry, Damon, I didn't mean to run off. I just didn't know what to do. I kind of panicked."

"It's okay, I understand. I shouldn't have just kissed you like that without even thinking of how it would make you feel."

"It felt amazing...well, until I panicked, then it didn't. But at first, it felt so good."

Damon's smile slowly spread across his face. Giovanni shouted from the back door something in Italian.

"Come on, let's go join them outside," he suggested.

I led the way out to the back patio. They had a fire going and marshmallows out to roast. Damon and I sat down next to one another. It was quiet as no one said anything. The fire crackling was the only sound.

"Well, what's going on?" Grace finally burst out, smiling.

Giovanni, who normally interrupted his wife when she was so bold, turned to look at us for a response. I looked at Damon, who then returned the look to me.

"We have decided to—"

"—take things slowly," Damon finished my sentence with a smile.

"So, you are dating?" Grace asked to clarify.

"Not yet," Damon smiled. "We are going to get to know each other first."

"But you are like perfect for each other, why—"

"Grace," Giovanni interrupted. "They gave their answer, let them be now."

She crossed her arms and stuck out her lower lip. "Fine," she pouted.

We sat for a while, toasting marshmallows and enjoying each other's company. As we were about to call it a night, Damon's phone pinged. His happy attitude faded instantly. The muscles in his shoulders tensed up. His smile disappeared as he pressed his lips into a tight line.

"There's someone at the front door. He's walking around the house now, south side."

Giovanni nodded and stood up. Damon got up, sticking his thumb against a box underneath the fire logs by the patio door and pulled out a gun.

"Hello?" the guy from the front door yelled. "Anybody out here?"

Damon threw Giovanni a gun and they quickly tucked them away.

"Back here," Damon yelled back.

The guy appeared from around the corner, greeting everyone with a smile.

"I'm sorry to interrupt, I know it's a little late. I'm looking for..." he looked at his hand, "Noelle Taylor."

"Girls, go inside," Damon said before I could answer.

I looked at Grace as my stomach flipped. Without a second thought I followed her back inside the house.

"Who sent you?" was all I heard Damon ask before we were out of earshot.

Grace and I anxiously waited in the living room for any kind of sign as to what was happening. Ten minutes later we saw the guy walk back to the front of the house. Grace and I heard the patio door open, then close. The guys came into the living room, sitting down in front of us.

"That guy was paid to deliver a letter to you," Giovanni told me. "Damon doesn't think you should read it, but in the end, that is your decision to make."

I looked back and forth between the three of them. "Did you read it?" I asked the guys.

They shook their heads. "It's from Austin," Giovanni added.

Damon wasn't speaking at all. I could tell something was bothering him. I looked at the envelope in Giovanni's hand. Half of me wanted to burn it, the other half was curious about what was in it. I reached out for it slowly. Damon took my hand, stopping me.

"Noelle, you don't want to read that letter. It is only going to upset and worry you. Please, it's not worth it."

"But I want to know what it says."

"It's probably an empty threat with a bunch of cruel words that no facts can back up. Trust me, it will only cause you more pain than anything."

I looked back at the envelope before finally shifting my gaze at Damon's pleading eyes. "I have to know what it says."

He ran his hands down his face as I took the envelope from Giovanni, tearing it open. Unfolding the paper in my shaky hands a picture fell into my lap. Flipping it over I saw a picture of Austin and me. I remembered the picture; it was taken when we were happy, before my parents died and I'd moved in with him. We were at the cookout of the summer. I was sitting on his lap, his arms firmly around me to claim me as his. I looked at my smile, so genuine and happy. My heart ached in remembrance of that time. I turned my attention to the letter.

We can be happy again, come back to me. We can start fresh like you never betrayed me. Please Noelle,

All the good times he was referring to flashed through my mind. There was a point in time we were happy, I wasn't denying that. But then the happy months turned into just a few weeks, then a couple days, and what we had landed on, before it all blew up, were only moments. These rare moments weren't going to grow back into those "good times" like he was implying. I clenched the paper in my hands. I reread the words that angered me again; 'we are all each other has now.' I had nothing left of my parents because of him. It wasn't my fault, nor was it Damon's; it was HIS. I grabbed the picture, slamming the letter down on the table in front of me before standing up to head out back. I could hear their footsteps close behind. Holding the picture out over the fire I began tearing it into tiny pieces. I watched as the pieces fell, igniting as they hit the flames. Grace was the first to speak, breaking the silence that had fallen over us.

"Can we read the letter?" she asked.

"If you want." I took a deep, calming breath. "Throw it the fire when you're finished—it's garbage. I'm going to bed."

I had just crawled into bed when a knock sounded.

"You can come in," I called.

Damon came through the door, walking over to sit on the edge of the bed. Reaching around he rubbed my back.

"You okay?"

"I'm just tired. I thought that when I left him it would be over... that I wouldn't have to worry about him anymore and could just be happy. I mean I figured he would be angry and come after me, but I didn't think it would escalate to him burning my store down." Tears started to form in my eyes. "I didn't think he would ever be this person. He's not the same man I fell in love with. Or maybe he is and I was just too blind to see it."

He tucked a loose strand of hair behind my ear.

"You know this isn't your fault, right?"

I nodded ever so slightly.

"Good. It'll get better, just take it one day at a time." He bent down, kissing my head. "I'm just down the hall if you need anything. Sweet dreams, beautiful."

I smiled to myself as he stood, walking out to leave me to my thoughts. It would get better. This was just the tough part. Eventually Austin would forget about me or give up, then I'd be free and happy again.

Chapter **Fifteen**

I WALKED DOWNSTAIRS THE NEXT MORNING TO Damon swimming in the pool out back. Grabbing a cup of coffee, I walked outside to greet him. He got out of the pool as I sat on a patio chair, his toned body glistening as the water fell from him.

"Morning you two!" Grace shouted as she walked toward us.

I smiled at her. "Morning, Grace."

"Where's Gio?" Damon questioned.

"In the shower." She turned to me. "Go out with me tonight?"

I paused. "Umm, last time we went out, I got into a fight. I don't think that's a good idea."

"Oh, come on, she had it coming. Plus, it was kind of Damon's fault. This time, the guys will be in town for work, so it'll be just us. It'll help get your mind off everything."

"How was it *my* fault?" Damon complained, as he grabbed a towel to dry off.

"Because if you didn't have random girls after you, it wouldn't have happened," she said, crossing her arms. "*That* makes it your fault."

Damon laughed, "Okay, I guess."

"I'll go…but I don't have anything to wear."

"Perfect excuse to go shopping! It will be so much fun!" she shrieked. "I'll go get ready, meet you in one hour."

She ran off to get ready, leaving me and Damon alone together.

"Come with me." Damon half-smiled, getting up to go inside.

I followed without question as he led me up to his room. I stopped at his door.

"You want me to come into your room?" I asked confused, then squinted my eyes at him in suspicion. "Explain yourself."

He laughed. "My office is through my room, that's where we are going."

I slowly began to follow him once more. Once in his office, he grabbed his computer and started typing. I waited patiently for whatever he was going to show me.

"Look," he stated.

I peered at the screen to see two photos of two men.

"Umm. Oh…kay…am I supposed to know them?" I chuckled.

"No, they will be following you and Grace tonight. They work for us and they are your protection. Just in case you see them following you, which you shouldn't, don't panic," he explained.

"By protection, you mean from Austin, right?"

He let out a small sigh. "I have to be honest with you, Noelle, because you need to know what you're getting into," he said.

I nodded for him to continue, not sure what to think.

"If you are involved with our family in any way—well, like I have said before, we have enemies." He paused, waiting for my reaction. "Those enemies will do anything to hurt our family and the business, even if that means going after a wife or girlfriend. So, you will always have someone assigned to protect you when you are out without myself or Gio." He paused, trying to read my face, then continued, "I understand if this is too much for you to live with, and I will understand it if, when the time comes, you choose not to get any more involved with me." There was a minute of silence between us. I reached up, hugging him against me.

"That changes nothing for me," I whispered. I felt his body relax into mine, pulling me tighter against him. I pulled away slowly realizing then that he was still shirtless. My eyes raked across his toned upper body. The hard lines of it a contrast to how smooth his skin appeared to be. Before I knew it, I had reached my hand out to run my fingers from his stomach up to his chest. I watched the goosebumps prick his skin, my touch leaving a trail of evidence. It wasn't until he used one finger to tilt my chin up to face him that I realized what I was doing. Mesmerized by him half nude in front of me I hadn't thought it through.

"You know, if you'd like to see the other half of me, that can be arranged." he teased with a wink.

I pulled my hands away, stepping backwards.

"I have to go get ready," I blushed turning to leave without another word.

His chuckle carried through his room.

"Me too, but I'd put off all my plans for you!" he called after me.

An hour and a half later, Grace and I were in the city. Our first stop was a coffee shop. I noticed she ordered two coffees. I asked her who the second one was for. She gave me a smile, saying it was for the guy following her for protection. I figured I'd do the same. I even tried to catch the guy grab the coffee, but by the time I looked back, it was already gone.

"Wow, they are good. I didn't see either of them."

Grace laughed. "That's the point. We don't see them, and they always see us."

I giggled as we walked downtown. We shopped for a couple hours, then met up with the guys for dinner. Damon sat next to me in the booth, placing his arm on the back of the seat.

"You girls having fun?" Giovanni asked.

"Yes. I got a ton of clothes to replace what I lost in the fire," I said. "I guess it is kind of refreshing, starting a new life without Austin, with new things."

After dinner, I hugged Damon before he jumped into Giovanni's car.

"So, slight change of plans. Gio and I have one more meeting and then we're going to meet you at the club. Does that sound good?"

"So, you're crashing our girls' night out?" I teased, giving him a smile. "I can't wait."

Grace and I headed straight to the club. It wasn't open yet, but the line was already forming outside the door. People began screaming at us as we walked in.

"Do you ever get used to that?" I asked.

"Not really. It's weird that people know your name, but you don't know them. Also, it's annoying how people think they are entitled to something because they know your last name."

"Oh, yeah, I can see how that would get annoying. Well, just something I'll have to get used to when Damon and I—" I paused as I saw the smirk on her face. "What?"

"You said *when*," she smiled. "If you were unsure, you would have said *if*. But you said *when*, which means you are planning on sticking with him."

She jumped up and down excitedly. I rolled my eyes and laughed. Inside, it was quiet with only the bartender talking to the DJ setting up across the room. She stopped and greeted us, getting Grace her usual and asking me what I wanted. After she handed me my order of Jack and Dr. Pepper, Grace turned to me.

"Want to see Damon's office?"

"Sure."

I followed her to the back, down a dimly lit hallway. She opened a door and I peered inside. Everything matched Damon's personality down to the leather chairs and two-seater couch to the right of the room. The entire wall behind his desk was filled with books. To the left, there was a pool table and door to a small closet. I sat down on the couch, taking a sip of my drink.

"Well, it is him, that's for sure," I smiled.

"You got that right! He and Gio designed their own offices. They connect through that closet, too, just in case they need to get to one place quick."

"Wow, I'm not sure whether that is cool or scary," I admitted. "But I like this office. It feels like I could just grab a book and read in here all night."

"I'm sure that's what he does when he has to stay late." She looked at her phone. "I'm going to get another drink before they open the doors so I don't have to wait in line when I finish this one. Want me to grab you one too?"

"Yeah, thanks."

I checked my phone. I had one missed call from a blocked number. Part of me wondered who it was, the other part didn't dare to find out. Grace came back with fresh drinks.

"The guys said they would be here in about twenty minutes," she said handing me a drink.

"Want to go dance?" I asked.

"Hell, yeah, I love dancing!" She smiled.

We made our way out to the dance floor. It was so relaxing to let loose and just move my body to the music. I was able to push the reminders of Austin and all the stress I had from losing the store to the back of my mind. I was in this moment with the music. The peace it brought me made me feel hopeful that this would soon become my new normal—from girl time with Grace to the freedom to enjoy myself at the club wearing whatever I wished.

One day I would have the ability to live how I wanted again and it was electrifying to imagine. It wasn't much longer before I felt someone come up close behind me, leaning into my ear.

"Miss me?"

I smiled as I immediately recognized Damon's voice. I leaned into him. We danced together for a long time before making our way to the side of the room. Sitting down in a booth across from Grace and Giovanni, we talked and laughed, just hanging out together the way people our age do all the time. I couldn't have been happier.

Eventually, a big guy in a black suit came over to the table. After Damon and Giovanni talked to him for a moment, they turned to us.

"My father is here, he wants to speak to us," Damon explained.

"All of us," Giovanni looked to Grace, taking her hand.

She gave him a nod before following behind him. I looked to Damon who had his hand out to me. I took it, letting him lead me to his office. Stefano greeted us all with a smile. I hugged him, still surprised at how comforting it was to suddenly have him in my life again.

"I have news," he stated, sitting on the front edge of Damon's desk. "A lead called me. Austin is planning to take Noelle in three days from an unknown location." He looked at me, and Damon squeezed my hand. "He is going to then contact us and insist that Damon come get her. When he does, a trap will be waiting. If his plan plays out, he will kill both of them." His voice appeared unfazed by the words he was speaking. I felt Damon's body tense up as he listened to his father's words. He let go of my hand, balling his fists at his sides. My heart was racing, and it felt as though the great night I was having was collapsing around me.

"However, we know of his plan and now we must act. And I am going to need everyone in this room to help." He looked to me again. "Do you know what plans you have three days from now? Be very specific."

"In three days," I thought aloud. "The anniversary of my parents' deaths."

I started, "Every year, since they were murdered, I do the same thing—go to the coffee shop in the morning, take an early shift at the bar, grab some flowers at the store next door, and then go to the cemetery. I stay there until the time of their death at 8:36 p.m. Then, Max meets me at the clearing and we drink while we watch the stars."

Stefano listened intently, hesitating like he was putting his thoughts together before speaking again.

Turning his attention to the guys, he started giving orders for his plan. "Gio, you and Damon will wait for the call from Austin. Grace," She nodded. "I need you to be with Noelle until the time comes. Then you will infiltrate the location with Damon and Giovanni, and since you are the best sniper out of the three of you, stay up high."

"Father—" Giovanni started.

"Gio, we do anything we can to keep our family safe. This is not only Noelle's life, but your brother's as well. I understand that you are worried, but Grace can handle it. You and Damon have both trained her to defend herself. The time has come for her to use the skills. Trust in her to get it done just as she trusts in you."

Giovanni looked at Grace. She put her hands on his face.

"It's okay, G, I will be fine." Her voice was soft and confident.

He locked his arms around her, not saying another word. Damon moved closer to me, almost like he was guarding me from the words his father was about to say.

"Noelle, you stick to your normal routine that day. Then, let Austin take you."

"Hell, no!" Damon said furiously, "There's no fucking way I'm going to just let him kidnap her. Your plan is shit, come up with a new one."

Stefano stood up, walking so he was inches away from Damon. The tension in the room was thick. "Son, I know you care deeply for her, but you have to let her do this. You may not like it, but it is ultimately her decision whether or not she goes through with it." He glanced at me.

I thought for a moment. Was I ready to finally face Austin? What if he tried to rape me again? What if he choked me again and didn't let go this time? Was I prepared for what he might have in store for me while I was alone with him? Yes, I was ready to begin my life without having to constantly look over my shoulder...without him. I would go through hell just to be rid of him. I looked to meet Damon's gaze. He saw the decision in my face.

"Noelle, we can come up with another plan. You are going to be alone with him for who knows how long. No one will be there to protect you. Please, let us do something else," he begged.

"Damon," I paused. "This is my battle. I am ready to face him one last time, but I want every detail of the plan from start to finish."

He begged me with his slate gray eyes, "Please." His voice was barely a whisper.

"I have to do this," I said softly.

He ran his fingers roughly through his hair, taking a step back from me. His jaw clenching and unclenching like he couldn't decide what to say. Then his hard eyes pierced mine. "No one will be there to protect you, Noelle. What if he hits you again? What happens when you are alone with him? What if we have bad information and he—what if he tries to—" He couldn't bring himself to say the words.

I knew what he was thinking, I had thought about it before making my decision. But I was stronger than I was weeks ago. Before I could say anything, Stefano started speaking again.

"Our information is not bad. It came from someone who cares deeply for Noelle."

Stefano walked to the door of the closet that connected to Giovanni's office. All our eyes were locked on the door. He paused before opening it to his source. The moment I saw him, I jumped over the chair next to me and ran to him. It was Max. He inhaled a deep breath.

"I have missed you so much, Noelle," he said.

He looked better than the last time I saw him. He still had all his facial hair, but he was getting back to his muscular body shape he had when he left.

"I will be there, at the location," Max said, looking past me to the others. "Austin is using some of Andres's men so it's common knowledge among the top guys about what is going down."

Stefano then explained the plan, from start to finish like I'd asked. But as Stefano was talking, Max's grip tightened around me.

"I don't like this plan. It puts her at high risk."

Damon nodded his head. "I agree. This is bullshit. I don't want her alone with him for any amount of time. She is walking into a very dangerous situation. There has to be a better way."

"We don't know the exact time she is being abducted or where they are taking her," Stefano explained. "If we knew that, then we could come up with a different plan, but we don't. This is the best we've got."

"Actually, there might be another way," Max stated.

I could tell the wheels were turning inside his head. "If I am able to tell you where they are taking her once they tell me, I can let Damon know. Then we can set up a reverse trap. But it will only work if we are somewhere close enough to beat them back to the location they're bringing her to. Then we can infiltrate and make sure all of Andres's men are taken care of, setting up our own people to be ready for when they do come."

"No one has said anything about where it could be?" Giovanni asked.

Max shook his head. "Not a thing, but I'm going to assume it's somewhere under Andres's control in the city."

"The club is closer to more of Andres's locations, we can wait here," Damon said.

Stefano nodded, "All right, Noelle will go about her day as usual. We will wait at the club for the message from Max, then move in. Grace, I still want you with Noelle then up high with a gun for backup just in case. Damon and Giovanni, you will wait with us here. When we get the location, everyone will report to where they need to go and we will get Noelle out safely."

Everyone agreed to the new plan. I was still nervous, but ready for it all to be over. As the silence took over, thinking about what was to come, my eyes flickered between Max and Stefano.

"How did you know to contact Stefano?" I asked. "Why didn't you call me?"

"He is the one who encouraged me to take this undercover position," Max admitted.

I turned my attention back to Stefano for an explanation. He crossed his arms over his chest saying nothing in response. The smirk that crossed his lips told me there was a relationship between them I was unaware of. I approached him, stopping a few feet in front of him. Mirroring his body language, I looked directly into his eyes.

"Why?"

"I needed someone who was close to you to infiltrate Montero's network."

"Why did it have to be someone close to me?"

He hesitated a moment before asking me to sit down.

"The last case your father worked on was against Andres Montero. I needed someone who understood the delicacy of the situation with the ability to investigate from the inside."

"What situation? Investigate what?"

"The person behind your parents' murder." Finally, uncrossing his arms, he walked around to sit in the desk chair across from me. "Max understood the situation from not only an officer's perspective but that of a close friend as well. He has the skills to investigate without being suspicious, and would contact me in case of any threat being made against you."

I shook my head. "Why would threats be made against *me*?"

"Noelle, that day in the court room when he was sentenced, Montero told your father he would do everything in his power to kill his entire family. Your father was a dear friend of mine and I promised to look out for you if something happened to him."

"But my dad was careful, he even took his wedding rings off when he worked on cases like this so people would assume he didn't have a wife or kids. There's no way to know I even existed."

"Noelle."

It was Max, his voice soft. He walked over, squatting down in front of me to look into my eyes.

"Austin works for Montero."

The dryness in my throat made my breath catch. My lower lip started to quiver.

"I met Austin before my dad took that case."

"I know, but Montero had been under investigation for years. He had to know the walls were closing in on him. There's not solid proof, but we think Austin was sent to keep an eye on your father."

I stood up, feeling sick to my stomach. My fingers tangled through my hair as I pulled it into a ponytail while I paced.

"Was any of it real?"

I never thought I would be sad over Austin no longer loving me. After all the abuse, I figured he hated me and had come to terms with it inside. But to find out it could have all been a ploy from the start just to get to my father made my heart break in two. The times he'd said he loved me in the beginning before he laid a hand on me, were those genuine? They felt like it to me. I'd fallen in love with him. Damon stepped in front of me to stop my pacing. I peered up at him.

"Is this real?" I whispered.

He slid his hand onto my cheek, staring straight into my eyes. He was not surprised by my question and didn't hesitate to nod.

"Yes."

The tears came then, like two streams flowing straight down my cheeks. He pulled me against his chest. Taking a deep breath, I untangled my arms from around Damon.

"Do you know who did it?" I asked Max.

"We have narrowed it down, but nothing solid."

I wished we could find the murderer. Then I could see him go to jail and have the closure I wanted. "Will you take me back to your place?" I asked Damon.

"Of course."

I hugged Max goodbye.

Chapter **Sixteen**

 pajamas, and crawled into bed. But I was wide awake, consumed with the tug-of-war my mind was having over if what Austin and I had was ever real. I was retracing every moment with him from the start. Each interaction I could remember I broke down. Was there ever a question he asked that was off-the-wall? Or about my father's work? Up until that day I couldn't recall him asking or doing anything in suspicion of studying my father.

Then my mind flickered to the look on Damon's face in the car. The ride home was quiet, Damon lost in thought. By the way he was gripping the steering wheel, they couldn't have been good.

With a heavy sigh I made my way along the dark hallway, the light peeking under Damon's doorway guiding me. I hesitated, knocking lightly.

"You can come in, Noelle."

I pushed open the door, halfway shutting it behind me. He was sitting on his bed, reading a book. I stopped next to his bed debating on climbing in with him or not. He waited a moment, setting his book aside, then patted the open spot next to him.

"What's up?" he asked, casually.

I suddenly couldn't form words. It was a weird feeling of nervousness as I sat next to him in his giant bed. I opened my mouth to try to say something but all I could choke out was, "Never mind."

He reached for my wrist lightly as I tried to climb back out of his bed. "Wait, talk to me."

His voice was calm. His gray eyes sucked me in. I could see he was as curious as I had been. I took a deep breath to calm my nerves.

"What were you thinking in the car?" I finally asked.

He looked down. "All the ways this could go wrong," he said softly. "I am trying to think of how this thing can go down so I can protect you in every situation possible."

"Three steps ahead?" I repositioned myself to face him. "It's going to be okay. I am going to be okay."

He winced. I took his hands, wrapping them around me as I straddled him. I hugged his neck, pulling him to me. We sat there for a minute in silence before I felt him shake his head. He pulled back to look at me, resting his hands on my lower back.

"Noelle..."

I looked into his eyes, seeing his desire. My eyes flickered between his eyes and lips as I leaned in closer to him. He met me halfway, pressing his lips onto mine. I grabbed a handful of his hair, pulling him closer. His hands traveled to my hips, stopping there but squeezing them lightly.

"Fuck, Noelle..." he whispered, breathless, as we parted.

I giggled as I pulled his shirt over his head. He wrapped his arm around my waist then flipped us over. I lay on my back, returning each kiss with just as much desire. But when he laced his fingers in mine, above my head, I flashed back to when Austin pinned me down that night.

"Stop!" I panicked, sitting up as Damon pushed himself off me.

I held my face in my hands, knowing I just ruined another moment between us that should have been so sweet and pure. "I'm sorry Damon, I—"

"Shhhh, it's okay, Noelle." He rubbed my back. "We don't have to do anything you don't want to do."

"It's not that I don't want to, I just—it took me back to when Austin—" I couldn't say those words again, shaking my head to myself. "I'm sorry."

He lifted my chin with two fingers. "You don't ever have to apologize to me for how you are feeling."

"But why does my mind go there when I know it's you and not him?"

He pulled me toward him, holding me close.

"Maybe you're not ready, Noelle. Your body may have healed but your mind takes a while longer. It's a response to my actions, not to me, and I know that. Give it time, we can take it slow. Let me hold you tonight, that's it. See if it helps."

His eyes were kind and encouraging. He waited for me to agree, then scooped me up under the covers. He paused.

"Do you want me to put my shirt back on?"

"No, it's okay."

His grin turned mischievous. "Oh, so you like what you see?"

That was just the sort of comic relief I needed as I felt a rush of relaxation spread through my body. I laughed at him.

"Eh, you're all right. I feel like I've seen better," I teased.

He smiled a goofy smile, pulling me closer to him. He lightly ran his fingers up and down my shoulder. I looked up at him.

"Thanks, Damon."

"For what?" he asked.

"Being patient with me."

He put his hand on the side of my neck. "Don't thank me, Noelle, this is how it's supposed to be when someone truly cares for you."

I smiled, laying my head on his chest. He kissed the top of my head once before I drifted off to sleep.

Damon didn't leave my side for the next two days. He was always there but never suffocating me. It felt so good to know someone had my back. The morning of the anniversary of my parent's deaths, he made me breakfast, bringing it up to his room where I had been sleeping since the news of Austin's plan came to light. I smiled at him, sitting up.

"You didn't have to do all this."

"I wanted to."

I laughed. "I don't think I really did anything that great to deserve this."

I could see the corners of his mouth twitch upwards in the slightest smile.

"Noelle," he cooed, his voice soft. "You are an amazing, beautiful woman. Any guy would be lucky to bring you breakfast in bed."

I could feel my cheeks heat up. I looked down at the plate of chocolate chip waffles.

"How did you know these are my favorite?" I asked, as he took a spot next to me.

"I might have asked Max what your favorite breakfast was...or maybe it was a lucky guess. We will never know." He winked.

He flipped on the TV as I ate. After breakfast, I walked downstairs, washing my dishes before placing them out to dry. It wasn't long before I was cleaned up and ready to go. I was walking toward the library when I noticed a bouquet of flowers in a beautiful vase sitting on the patio table outside the sliding-glass door. They were the exact flowers I bought for my parents every year since they died. I looked around outside before reaching for the handle. I didn't see anyone. I unlocked the door, opening it to step out.

"Noelle!" Damon yelled desperately from upstairs.

I turned to face him as he ran toward me, a gun in his hand. My body felt like it was concrete. I couldn't move, paralyzed in fear. He reached out, touching my cheek.

"Go into the library, type in three-zero-six-five in the keypad inside the door to the right."

"Wha—"

"Noelle, go. Three. Zero. Six. Five," he snapped, his voice sharp.

I ran to the library doing exactly what he said. After I typed in the code, a sheet of metal came down, covering the door and windows. When it clicked into place, I listened quietly. It felt like an eternity before the metal sheets started to rise again. I stepped back into the furthest corner of the room before crouching down.

"Noelle?"

It was Damon. I stood up, running to him. He hugged me against him tightly as all the emotion came crashing out of me as my body shook. It was like the crash of a bad adrenaline rush.

"It's okay." He kissed the top of my head, rubbing my back lightly.

"What happened?"

When I pulled back to look at him, he avoided my eyes for a moment. His weight shifting from one foot to another. He was debating on whether to tell me everything or tell me not to worry about it.

"I want to know," I whispered.

"Okay," he sighed. "Someone tried to get in through the back door. My camera picked them up, which they then saw and took off. I wasn't sure if they were going to come with backup or not. They left you the flowers. There's a card attached. Do you want to read it?"

I nodded, lacing my fingers with his as he led me out to the living room. Giovanni and Grace were there. She was looking out one window, a gun tucked into the back of her jeans. Giovanni was checking the other one. He handed me the small card still in the envelope.

"You didn't read it first?" I asked them.

"No, go ahead, but read it out loud, please," Damon asked, sitting on the table across from me.

I opened the card, reading it to myself first.

I know they know. The clearing, 15 minutes, alone, or they all die.

I swallowed hard, feeling all the blood leave my face.

"See you soon, Austin," I lied.

I put the card back into the envelope and slid it into my back pocket. "I think—" I paused, "I think I need a minute alone."

Damon nodded, standing with me. He pulled me into a hug before I took a step. I felt him inhale deeply, then exhale against me.

"We will get him, Noelle, then you will be free to do as you wish without having to worry about anything. I will never let him hurt you again."

When he pulled back, I put my hands on either side of his face. My lips pressed against him in a kiss that I desperately didn't want to end. I tried to put all the deep emotion—dare I say it, love—I felt for Damon into the kiss.

I looked into his eyes, a tear leaking from my own. "I'm sorry." His brows tugged together in confusion, not only by the depth of my kiss but my words afterwards.

"You don't have to apologize, it's not your fault. He is the one attacking you and we are all aware of what we need to do to protect you. We want to help you, Noelle."

I looked down at the floor before walking up to my room. I shut the door behind me, trying to think of a way to get out without them noticing. Or should I just stick to the plan? I paced in my room for five minutes, glancing between the card and out the window. If I went, then I could protect them all. This was my problem. Austin was mine to deal with. If I didn't go, I knew Austin would kill them, or at least try to kill them. After everything he'd done, I knew his threats were not empty. Was I willing to chance their lives to stick to the plan I wasn't sure would even work? He already knew they had figured it out. That meant he could have altered his original plan and they would go in blind, making them even easier to take by surprise. I couldn't risk their lives.

My eyes ticked back to the window. Could I survive the drop from the window? What if I jumped into the pool? Would I be fast enough to climb out before they got to me? I checked the clock again, nine minutes left to get there. As I opened the window to get a better look at how far down the drop was, I heard them walking out to the patio. *Perfect,* I thought to myself, *I can walk right out the front door.* I dropped everything, running down the stairs and out the front door. I didn't stop until I got to the clearing.

I checked the time again, two minutes to spare. No one was there. I looked out across the water below.

"Ahh, finally, you came to your senses."

My entire body tensed. I turned to face Austin. He had someone with him. A giant of a man, at least a foot taller than Austin, with broad shoulders. He was bald and had scruff where a beard would be. His eyes stared holes into my skin. Wearing a suit, he stood with his arms clasped together in front of him, ready for his orders.

"What do you want?" I blurted out.

He chuckled. "You."

Charging toward me, he grabbed a fistful of my hair. Yanking it backward, he planted a kiss on my exposed neck.

"You resist, you feel pain. It's just that easy, got it?"

I attempted to nod. "Yes."

"Here is what you are going to do. You are going to call Damon and tell him you choose me. You are going to tell him that he was never man enough for you like I was. You never want to see him again. Then we can begin our journey to our happily ever after."

I nodded, calling Damon on my phone.

"Noelle? Where did you go, are you okay?"

"Damon, I—I'm sorry but I choose Austin."

"What?"

"I want t—to be with Austin, n-not you," I stuttered.

"Is he there right now? Where are you?"

I could tell he was panicking. My heart twisted in pain for him.

"Yes, Damon," I said, trying to disguise my true answer. "It's best if you let me go. I'm sorry." I looked to Austin, knowing I had to say this before he killed me, "I think I love you, Damon. I'm sor—"

A punch met my head, knocking me to the ground. My vision blurred as I saw Austin picking up my phone from the ground.

"Grab her, Scott, we're leaving."

He then began talking to Damon as I was lifted from the ground. I was carried to a car waiting for us only a side trail away. They threw me in the trunk as everything went black.

I opened my eyes slightly, letting the light peek through. My head was throbbing. My hands were tied above my head to a pipe in the ceiling. My toes barely touched the ground. I tried to look around, hearing someone come closer to the door.

Austin walked in with Scott, who was holding a phone. Austin had a knife in his hand.

"How—how did you know about the clearing?" I asked weakly.

He laughed. "Oh please, Noelle, I knew you went there every day. I just never knew why you waited for me to go to work before you ran there."

I didn't answer, I couldn't. It would only make him angrier. I felt myself shutting down.

"Dial it. On video chat so we can see his face," Austin ordered Scott. "Maybe you won't talk to me, but I know you will talk to him."

"Bastard, where did you take her?" I could hear Damon yell.

"Shh, my turn to do the talking, Mr. Amoretti." He smiled, showing his knife to the camera. "I would hate for this to slip," he said, putting the knife against me. He dug the knife into my side. I let out a yelp of pain.

"You son of a bitch!" Damon screamed.

The phone was facing me. I could see the torment in his face. Austin laughed once before turning back to Damon.

"Here is the deal, Damon. Noelle and I were going to run away together. However, with her confessing her feelings for you, I have no other choice but to kill her. But," he paused, "since I am a full believer in love," he said sarcastically. "You have approximately thirty minutes to save her. At the thirty-one-minute mark, I will call you again, and you will then watch her die. Do we have a deal?"

"Deal."

"Great, now if you will excuse us, I am going to make sure Noelle has the best thirty minutes of her life."

He ripped open my shirt.

"Noelle—"

Scott hung up and walked out of the room, leaving me alone with Austin. My heart was beating so hard in my chest I felt it in my ears. The anticipation of what was to come made my breaths quicken. I wondered if he was really going to give him thirty minutes or just kill me now. He paced for a few minutes, almost like he was debating something.

"Sad thing is, in thirty-one minutes, after I kill you, I'm going to kill him just like the original plan."

Then he stopped inches from my face. He kissed me, smashing his lips hard against mine. I tried to pull back, but couldn't move. He untied my arms from the pipe, keeping my wrists tied together. My knees felt weak as my body weight hit the floor. Austin caught me before I fell, pushing me against the wall. His hand began to roam my body, stopping at my breasts.

"Please, Austin, don't."

He pushed me down onto my knees, unzipping his zipper.

"You bite me, I kill you." He pressed the knife against my neck.

He shoved himself inside my mouth, grabbing a handful of my hair tightly. Tears streamed down my cheeks. I gagged a few times, only encouraging him to shove deeper into my throat. He moaned my name, telling me how much I deserved this. Once he finished, he threw me to the concrete floor.

"I'll be back in fifteen minutes for the real fun," he smirked, pausing at the door. "You know, I'm not sure what Damon sees in you. You are a broken piece of trash no one would want...you stupid bitch."

I cried on the cold floor, broken just like he said I was. He was going to kill me; I might as well accept it. But did I want to endure the rest of the pain he was going to put me through? I looked at the rope on the floor. My eyes flashed to the chair. No, I had to fight back. I had to show Austin once and for all I was even stronger than when I walked out on him that night. I placed the chair behind the door. I grabbed the remaining rope and stood on the chair, waiting. I tried to make a wide circle with the rope though my wrists were still tied together, my adrenaline growing each moment it was quiet.

I heard a slight commotion outside the door. This was it. My brain frantically trying to go through all the possible outcomes of what I was about to do and if it would even work. I shook away the thoughts of failure and got ready to pounce. As the door swung open, I launched toward him, wrapping the rope around his neck from behind. I pulled backward, tightening the rope.

Chapter **Seventeen**

I froze—it wasn't Austin's voice. I dropped the rope taking a step back. It was Max who turned to face me. He took a step forward, a small, sad smile on his face.

"There's the fighter I grew up knowing!" He smiled a little bigger, pulling me in for a hug. He pulled a knife from his pocket, releasing my wrists from their rope. He hugged me again, this time I was able to put my arms around his neck.

"Are you okay?" He took a step back to examine me.

"How did you find me?" I ignored his question.

"A source within the organization, who isn't fond of Austin using Montero's resources to taunt the Amoretti family for personal gain."

"Where is he?"

"He bolted. We will find him though, don't worry. This ends today. Now answer me, are you okay?"

"I just want to go home, and I want him out of my life."

"Noelle, all the things he did to you. Why didn't you ever tell me?" His expression turned to sad pain for only a moment. "I could have helped you."

I shook my head. "Max I—" I paused, not able to get everything out fast enough. "I was scared, and now look. I'm in this position because I left. He burned down the bookstore and my apartment above it and—"

"Shhhh, it's okay," he whispered. "I know—I know, Noelle."

After a minute of silence, Max laced his fingers with mine.

"Ready to get out of here?"

I nodded, giving his hand a squeeze. He led me through the maze of hallways and stairs until we were at the ground floor of a warehouse. I could see the exit door from where we were standing. All of a sudden, about thirty feet away from the door, a man came out of nowhere and tackled Max. I screamed as he yelled to me.

"*Run*, Noelle!"

I debated—do I run away, or help him? I stood there, watching as the two men exchanged punches on the ground. The guy was on top of Max, returning every punch Max was giving. Something inside me couldn't take it anymore. I took off, charging toward the man pummeling Max. I lowered my shoulder and rammed into him as hard as I could. He tumbled over with a thud. He swung his arm back to punch me, but I escaped his reach. I ran back toward Max who was getting up as quick as he could. He moved in front of me.

"Noelle, what the hell? I said run!" he yelled, not meeting my eyes, raising his fists as the guy came toward him.

"I can't leave you," I explained. "I can't—"

"Yes, you can." He glanced back at me for only a second before yelling, "Now go! I'll see you outside." He growled, "after I take care of this dumbass."

I turned to run, sprinting toward the door. I flung it open, running outside only to smack right into Austin. It was like he was waiting for me. He grabbed a handful of the front of my shirt, yanking me back inside. Austin yelled at the man fighting Max. He immediately backed off and retreated to Austin's side. Max looked both slightly surprised and angry. His knuckles were swollen and bloodied. Austin threw me to the ground at Max's feet. I stood up, standing close to him.

Austin laughed. "I figured you would show up sooner or later."

Max didn't say anything, only checked his watch.

"Only too bad," Austin taunted. "Too bad you can't save her. Tell me, why do you have such an interest in her well-being? She is a pathetic bitch with no home."

I could see Max's hands ball into fists. "Fuck you, Austin. You don't know shit."

"Oh, I see what it is," he said, smiling. "She's giving it up to you both, isn't she? You *and* Damon?" He looked at me.

Max took a step forward ready to give Austin a piece of his mind and fist. I could see his jaw clenching. Austin put his hands up, causing Max to stop.

"Ah, wait a second and think this through, Maxwell," he teased. "There are two of us and one of you. How do you think you are going to protect that slut while fighting with one of us?"

Max's alarm on his watch went off. His entire body relaxed a little bit and I actually saw him smirk.

"What makes you think I came here alone?" he asked.

A look of panic crossed Austin's face. He looked around, paranoid. The tension in the room was thick and a slight noise from behind me caused me to jump. I reached out to touch Max's arm, scared to turn to see who was there.

"It's okay, Noelle," a calming voice whispered.

I must have been holding my breath because I let out the air as I turned to see him. He had a gun in one hand, the other was reaching out to me. I clung to both him and Max while Austin processed what was happening. But instead of showing any kind of concern or fear, he started laughing.

"I fucking knew it!" he laughed. "She is giving it up to both of you. I knew you were a whore all along. You just didn't want me in on the action. So, I had to take it, of course," he snickered. "Did I tell you we also had a little fun after we called you, Damon? We couldn't help ourselves, she begged me for it and who can say no to having that pretty little mouth around your dick?"

"You're disgusting," Damon said, staring at Austin. "Trust me when I say this, it will be my pleasure to see this through."

He tucked his gun behind his back, looking at me.

"Go with Max, Noelle, please," he begged. "You don't need to see this."

He wiped a tear from my cheek. I didn't realize I was crying.

"I'll meet you at the spot when we're done here, I promise," he whispered.

I looked to Max, who nodded. No matter how much I wanted to see this through, I knew they were right. I gave Damon's hand a squeeze as I turned to walk away with Max.

"Don't you want to take this with you, Noelle? After all, it was your father's," Austin's voice was calm and calculated.

I froze. My eyes moved to glance at Max who spun around to see what Austin was referring to. Slowly, I turned around. Austin stood there smiling, his hand extended. Hanging from his fingers was a small black pouch. It was my father's, I recognized it. I took a step forward only to have Max stop me.

"Wait," he ordered, not looking away from Austin. "Toss it here."

Austin tossed it to Max's feet. I watched Austin's face carefully, trying to read it for clues as to what he had up his sleeve. Something wasn't right; I could feel it in my gut.

"Noelle," Max's voice was merely a whisper as I finally broke my stare from Austin.

There, sitting in Max's palm, were my parent's wedding rings. Anger began to rage inside me. I snapped my eyes back to Austin.

"You had these the entire time? You knew how hard it crushed me when it was reported they were stolen after they were kil—" My face twisted. "How did you get these?"

Austin let out a laugh. "Isn't it obvious, you stupid cunt?"

I stared at him trying to wrap my head around it. He cocked his head sideways, as if inspecting me.

"It was me," he said proudly.

Red—that was all I saw as I launched myself toward him. I felt Max's arms around my waist trying to hold me back. Austin was laughing at me; he had been laughing at me for years. I wiggled out of Max's hold only to have Damon block me from Austin. He wrapped his arms around me in a tight hug.

"Let me go!" I screamed.

While my arms were around Damon, I felt the handle of his gun. I took a full deep breath. I made peace with what I was about to do.

"If I let you go, are you going to run at him?" he asked.

I wasn't, I had something else in mind. I made sure I looked Damon in the eyes before responding.

"No, I am not going to run," I answered.

The moment I felt his grip loosen, I grabbed Damon's gun and pointed it firmly at Austin. The guy next to him drew his own gun. He had it aimed at me for only a moment before Austin ordered him to put it away. He had a cockiness in his voice that bothered me.

"Noel—" he began.

"No!" I yelled at him taking a step forward. "You don't get to talk now. It's my turn."

"Noelle, please don't do this," Max said softly.

"He killed my parents, Max. Then he told me he loved me. I believed him. I kissed him and told him how much I loved him. I gave him *everything*—I—"

"It's not your fault," Damon interjected. "You didn't know. Give me the gun and I will take care of everything."

I started to crack, slightly lowering the gun.

"Aww, poor Noelle, always the victim," Austin teased. "I tell you what, I am so happy to finally be done with your whiny ass. What's wrong, can't be a big girl for once in your worthless life?"

I straightened up, pointing the gun right back at him. But when I saw that pleased smile on his face something inside of me caused me to freeze. I had just given him the reaction he'd wanted. All it did was show him he still had power over me. Our entire relationship had led up to him controlling my every move. Leaving him should have ended that, yet as I stood before him in that warehouse reacting to his words like he planned, I was showing him he was still in control over me—over my actions and emotions, my paranoia that made me constantly look over my shoulder, everything. When would it stop? I swallowed hard, steeling myself. It stopped now!

"I am not a victim." I gritted my teeth, my hand clutching the gun so tightly it shook. "I am a survivor...and I will not let your words have any more power over me."

I lowered the gun, handing it to Damon. My reaction was not one Austin had expected or wanted. It angered him and the blind rage he had gave him the confidence to stalk toward me.

Damon cut him off, pressing the gun against his forehead. "Don't give me the pleasure, you piece of shit."

Austin put his hands up, taking a step back. His eyes darted back and forth from me to Damon, appearing to debate on lunging for me or not. Damon stepped in front of me to block him.

"Max, I'm ready to take her home."

Max touched his finger to his ear, saying just a single word, "Go." Police officers came flooding through the area, surrounding us. Their guns were drawn and they yelled at Damon to drop his gun. Why were they yelling at Damon? He was the one who was preventing Austin from doing anything to hurt me. Did they not know? Everyone was shouting and my body started to come down from the adrenaline. Damon did as they said and the officers swarmed Damon and Austin, putting them both in cuffs.

"I'll be out in five years, this isn't over Noelle," Austin snarled.

"Wait!" I called to the officers walking him out.

They paused, looking back at me. I walked over to face him.

"You're going to be charged with first degree kidnapping. The minimum sentence for that is twenty years. Combine that with the fact that you confessed to murdering my parents, and you are looking at prison for the rest of your life." My fists clenched as my anger grew. "Remember, there are consequences to every action. Make sure you tell Andres hello for me."

Austin growled, trying to pull away from the officer who had a hold of him.

"I should have just killed you, you bitch!" he yelled.

Max moved between us, signaling for the officer to continue leading Austin away. He turned toward me.

"I'm glad that you still have that fire in you. I've said that once, but I just want you to hear it again." He smiled, "Now let's get you looked at."

He brought me outside to an ambulance to get checked out. He was right; I did still have that burning fire inside. Austin had tried to smother it, yet I felt a new confidence after standing up to him.

"Can I have my parents' wedding bands?"

His face fell.

"They're evidence, Noelle. I have to turn them over."

"Oh."

My heart broke, they were the last pieces I had of my parents after losing the store. Max took my hand.

"I will get them released back to you the moment the trial is over and they are done with them."

"Promise?"

He nodded. "I promise."

A rogue tear fell down my cheek. I wiped it away before anyone could notice.

"Are you going to be all right while I get Damon out of cuffs?" he asked.

I nodded, being taken care of by the EMS worker. He cleaned and wrapped the cut on my side. Giovanni and Grace walked over to join me as I waited.

"Where were you two?" I asked.

"Behind you, just out of sight," Giovanni smiled.

Damon walked over, rubbing his wrists.

"Are you all right?" I asked taking his hands to inspect his wrists.

He gave me a smile. "More than all right. Ready to go home?"

"Yeah."

He grabbed my hand and walked with me to the car. We got in and I buried my head into his shoulder. It wasn't long before we were on the way home.

"He is never going to hurt you again. Time for you to live your life like you want to," he whispered as he rubbed my back.

I fell asleep in his arms before we reached his house.

Chapter **Eighteen**

I WOKE UP IN DAMON'S BED THE NEXT MORNING. THE spot where he slept was empty. The previous day felt like a dream. I heard laughter from downstairs. I got up to investigate, walking down the stairs quietly. Damon, Giovanni, and Grace were all in the kitchen. Damon came to me immediately.

"How do you feel?"

"Tell me it wasn't all just a nightmare?" I said.

He smiled. "It was not. Although I wouldn't consider it a complete nightmare since you stood up to him the way you did. That took a lot of strength and I admire that in you."

I smiled back, my cheeks turning a light shade of pink. "I just—it was time for me to take back the control he stole from me."

"You took it back, all right. He's going to be locked up for a long time, if not for the rest of his life."

It felt like a weight was lifted off my shoulders. I was excited and determined to start this new life without Austin. Yet the more

I thought about what had happened, what Austin had taken from me, the more I felt sick to my stomach. Damon reached out to touch my shoulder.

"What are you thinking?" Damon asked, trying to read my expression.

"I, um..." I shook my head taking a step away. "I'll be back later."

"Wait," he called after me. I froze, my body tensing as I turned to face him. Was he going to tell me no? Or demand he go with me? My eyes slid up to meet his. He approached me slowly, seeing my reaction to his one-word order. He gave me a hug and planted a soft kiss on my cheek. There were no directions to follow except for one, which he said with a small smile.

"Be careful."

Not hesitating, I ran upstairs to grab a small blanket and my wallet. I threw them into a bag, heading out the front door. My first stop was getting a coffee, as I knew I was going to be out there for a while. Then to the flower shop, buying a giant bouquet of flowers. Finally, I walked to the cemetery. I fluffed out the blanket in front of my parents' headstone, setting the flowers gently against it. I sat down, staring at the large rectangular white stone pillar with their names. I took a sip of my coffee, tapping the lid with my finger as I thought back on everything that had happened since the last time I was here.

"I'm sorry I didn't make it yesterday." My voice was weak. "Can I tell you what happened?"

I paused, taking another sip of my coffee.

"Maybe I should start from the day I asked you and mom for

help at the clearing. You remember that? When I asked you for a sign?" I smiled a little. "The fact that you plopped Stefano's son into my life shortly after makes me think you two had planned on introducing us one day all along...or maybe you didn't. It happened, though," I paused, looking down at my coffee as my smile fell. "A lot has happened."

Not sparing any detail, I told them everything that had happened from the moment I asked for their help to me sitting in front of them in this cemetery. My emotions were a roller coaster, and I had to stop a few times to calm myself as I sobbed in front of them. I lay on my side, curling into a ball.

"I'm really feeling kind of lost despite all of this new freedom I suddenly have," I continued, as I took a deep breath. "It's like my mind knows I'm safe yet my body still has these reactions as if he's still free to come after me. The first thing I felt today was excited he was gone. It was only a momentary thought, and then I felt an overwhelming pit growing in my stomach. Yesterday keeps replaying in my mind." My tears began once more. "The fact that he thought he could just do whatever he wanted to me makes me sick. I feel so dirty—I scrubbed and scrubbed my body this morning, yet I still feel disgusting. How do I make that feeling go away?"

I was exhausted; I closed my eyes for a moment. A deep sigh escaped from my lips as I focused on my breathing.

Cold, wet drops of water splashed on my cheek. I flinched, opening my eyes. It was dark and I realized I must have fallen asleep. I peered up at the dark sky as the rain started to come down heavier. I sat there, staring at their headstone for who knows how long. I was drenched from head to toe but wasn't ready to leave yet. Then suddenly, the rain stopped. I looked up, seeing an open umbrella above my head. I turned, seeing Damon smile at me. When I didn't get up, he crouched down to me.

"Would you like me to leave you with the umbrella, or may I join you?" he asked.

I nodded, smiling up at him.

"You know," he started as he sat down. "I was trying really hard not to panic when it got dark."

I half-smiled. "Sorry."

"It's okay, I just wanted to make sure you were safe."

"How did you figure out I was here?"

"I implanted you with a chip. It tracks your location."

His attempt to keep a straight face failed miserably as he laughed.

"So, Max told you," I guessed.

"Yeah. I mean I checked at the clearing and then called to see if you were at his house." He sighed. "I wasn't trying to come after you or anything, I just wanted to make sure you were safe."

I leaned my head on his shoulder. "I know."

He let the silence fall between us until I was ready to go back to his house. He'd brought towels, thinking I was at the clearing. I dried off in the front seat of his jeep as best I could. The towels were warm and soft, and felt good against my cold skin.

After a hot shower, I put on pajamas and shuffled down to where Damon was in the basement. He was watching TV, his eyes locking on to me as I moved through the room. Taking a blanket from the other couch I curled up next to him. He reached up to put his arm around my shoulders. I threw up my arm, flinching as I shielded my face. It was only after the reaction had happened that my mind caught up with the reality of the situation. My eyes started to water. I hate that this had become some kind of messed up reflex. I saw how much it upset him by the look in his eyes.

"I'm sorry," I said, as my lower lip quivered.

"It's okay, can I hold you?"

My nod was slight but he saw it. Lying back on the couch, he opened his arms for me to move into them, giving me the control. I crawled into his arms, burying my face in his chest. His movements were slow as he reached an arm around me to rest his hand on my back. I cried into his chest, profusely apologizing as he told me repeatedly there wasn't a need to do so.

"Look at me, Noelle," he whispered.

I did, meeting his eyes as they peered into mine.

"Please tell me deep down you know I would never lay a hand on you."

"I know."

He seemed relieved, running his fingers through my hair. I closed my eyes, feeling it calm me as I took a deep breath. I snuggled my way closer, pressing my face against his chest once more.

Chapter **Nineteen**

TWO MONTHS LATER I STOOD IN THE AISLE OF THE bookstore I had dragged Damon into. He'd brought me to the city again for a date and this store caught my eye. I stared at the row of books in front of me. All of them study guides for the LSAT, the law school entrance exam. Damon had been looking at books in Italian. I pulled a study guide from the shelf, reading the jacket that explained all the extras it came with. It'd been a constant debate whether or not I wanted to pursue a law career like my father, but recently I'd had the urge to go for it. Maybe it was because Austin's trial started soon and I knew I'd have to testify against him. Having a deeper understanding of laws and rights could help me be prepared.

"Get it," a voice encouraged.

I turned to see Damon, a book in his hand.

"I don't know."

"What's stopping you?"

"I—" I looked back down at the book. "I want to make my dad

proud. What if I don't get a good score or don't get accepted to law school?"

He put one hand lightly on my back. "I have no doubt that your parents would be proud of you with whichever path you choose, no matter the outcome. Besides, I could use a good lawyer."

I laughed. "That wouldn't be a conflict of interest."

"Hey, I can be professional when I need to be." He stepped closer to me, leaning into my ear to whisper, "Can you?"

His breath on my skin still never failed to give me goosebumps, sending a tingle down my spine. I giggled, stepping away, but reaching out to take his hand.

"I'll get it, but I don't know if I'm going to pursue anything yet."

He shrugged, muttering, "That's fair."

After the bookstore, we drove to a tall dark gray building. Damon pulled into the valet area, walking around to get my door and helping me out.

"This looks like a hotel."

"It *is* a hotel."

"Are we staying the night? We don't live that far."

He laughed. "No, we are going up to the roof."

"Why?"

"That's where we're going to eat."

"On the roof?" my eyes went wide.

He laced his fingers through mine with a smile, leading me to the elevator. We stepped out to a long hallway. It had maroon carpeting and ended with two glass double doors. Stepping through them we were greeted by a hostess.

"Do you have a reservation?"

"Yes, Damon Amoretti."

The woman looked down the list, picking up two menus from the counter behind her before turning back to us.

"Right this way."

We followed her out to the patio, which was, in fact, on the roof. We sat at a table off to the side. I looked out at the view of the city. It was a breathtaking sight; one I didn't want to tear my eyes from.

"What is it?" Damon asked, noticing.

"This place seems so familiar but I know I've never been here before."

"No, but you pointed it out that first time we came to the city. Remember? I told you I'd bring you back here."

"You are a man of your word," I said, raising my glass.

"Well, you make me want to be the best man I can be," he said, in turn.

I looked down at the gorgeous table setting and tried not to blush. It amazed how he could still make my heart flutter with just his words. Thankfully, our server came with our meals.

"Noelle?" he got my attention while we ate.

"Hmm?"

When I looked up, I saw how nervous he was and that made me worried. I reached across the table to take his hand.

"What's wrong?" I asked, alarmed.

"Nothing is wrong," he said with a smile. "I just—I wanted to ask you if we could, maybe label what we are now?"

I blushed unintentionally, wondering if I was ready. But we'd basically been dating since everything went down. Maybe even sometime before that, I didn't know, the past was messy.

"So, you are asking me to be your girlfriend?"

"Yes."

"I'm okay with that."

His smile widened. "Really?"

I nodded, seeing that smile turn goofy as we continued eating. As the sun began to go down, the string lights on the patio flipped on to illuminate the area around us. The waitress brought out dessert for us to share. I glanced around the area, taking in its beauty. We moved to the side of the patio after dinner.

"This was perfect, Damon," I beamed at him. "Thank you."

He kissed my cheek. "I'm pretty sure it was mutually beneficial."

"Oh yeah?" I giggled. "How so?"

"I got a girlfriend out of it."

"Oh?" I asked in mock surprise.

"Yeah, I couldn't believe it either. She's damn beautiful, strong, and the most...spicy woman I've ever met."

"Spicy?"

"Like a damn jalapeno."

I laughed, leaning against him. He moved his arm to reach around my shoulders. I didn't flinch. I still had some moments where I wasn't sure how to react, but he'd been so patient with me. He never stopped encouraging me to react however I felt in the moment, knowing my body would eventually heal to where it would no longer happen.

We sat like that until the sun disappeared in the sky.

As we arrived home—*home*, that was another thing I was still getting used to, a real place to call home—there was a wooden crate sitting next to the front door.

"It's finally here!" Damon said.

"What is?" I asked.

Damon picked up the crate like it weighed nothing, while I unlocked the door. "Come on, I'll show you."

I followed him into the living room, where he set the hefty box down on the floor. He was beaming, like a kid on Christmas morning. "I'll be right back, stay here."

"Okay," I said, his excitement growing contagious.

He jogged off toward the garage, and came back with a crowbar. He pried up the nailed-on lid of the crate, working his way around the sides, until he could lift off the top.

I leaned over to peek inside, but it was filled to the top with foam packing peanuts. "What is it?" I asked again.

Damon smiled as he reached both arms into the box, and slowly pulled out smaller box, which he sat down on the floor in front of me. "Open it."

"Me?" I asked, pointing at my own chest.

"Yes, you," he said, laughing.

I lifted the lid and I immediately recognized it. My hand flew to my mouth, tears springing to my eyes. "I can't believe you did this. I can't believe you remembered!" I shrieked. "So, this—this is really ours?"

"No. It's yours," he corrected, reaching into the smaller box to set the sculpture on the coffee table, so that I was at eye level with my little white elephant.

I threw my arms around his neck, my stream of tears falling on to his shoulder.

"This means your happy, right?" he asked.

I kissed him deeply, pulling him closer to me.

"I'll take that as a—" he breathed, in between kisses. "As...a...yes."

"Yes," I finally said, wiping my tears and looking into his eyes. "This sculpture—this gift—it means so much to me."

We sat there together for I don't know how long, just admiring my new artwork—this tiny elephant, finding the strength to fight her way free. When I turned to look at Damon, he was already watching me, smiling.

He was brave and asked me something tonight at dinner that had been on his mind. Now it was my turn.

"So, now that we're officially *official*," I started. "Can I ask you something I've been thinking about?"

"Anything," he replied.

"Will you teach me how to defend myself like Grace?"

His expression turned hesitant.

"Are you sure you are ready for that?"

"I want to learn."

"I know, and I will teach you, yes, but when you're ready. Are you ready for someone to take a swing at you?"

I ran my fingers through my hair. "I don't know, but I want to try. Please? I want to feel strong again. I feel like I have control over my decisions now, maybe not all my reactions, but I can tell it's getting better. I just want to see what happens."

His silence filled the room. I could tell he was debating on whether or not it was a good idea. I knew there may be a chance that I'd flinch, but there was also a chance I would fight back instead.

"Okay, but I want you to tell me if you feel overwhelmed or have flashbacks or feel in any way like how you did with him. Then we are taking a break for a bit."

"Deal."

The next morning, I woke with a new level of determination. I wanted to do things as I wished and that started with Damon and me. With a boost of confidence, I got dressed and made my way to find him. He was in his office and the confidence I had quickly dwindled as I heard him yelling at someone on the phone. It was in Italian, but I could tell he was angry. When he slammed the phone down, I jumped. I'd never seen him this angry before. He rubbed his face with his hands, taking a deep breath.

"You can come in, Noelle."

I hadn't realized he saw me. I stepped inside feeling the tension of his conversation through the room. He looked at me, waiting for me to say something but I didn't.

"Never mind," I stated moving towards the door. "I can come back."

"Wait." He got up, walking toward me.

He took my hands, pulling them around his neck before hugging my waist. I heard him take another deep breath, inhaling me as he buried his face into my damp hair. I gave him a slight squeeze, feeling him relax in my arms.

"I'm sorry," he said, pulling away. "You can talk to me when I'm mad, it's okay. I won't take it out on you." He kissed my cheek. "What's up?"

"I um—I wanted to talk to you about our relationship."

His hands dropped from around me and he took a step back. The worry in his eyes was obvious, though he tried to hide it.

"What about it?" he asked, forcing a smile. "You're not having second thoughts already, are you?"

"No." I shook my head. "I want it to be equal."

His brows furrowed now. "Equal?"

"Yeah, I want to help pay for things, the bills and stuff. Either that or I can find my own place if you'd rather do that."

"No," he answered quickly. "I like you here with me, I don't want you to go. But I bought the house, I don't have a mortgage on it."

"You have water, trash, electricity, Internet, and groceries," I noted. "I want to help. I want this to be an equal relationship where we both put into it. I don't want to just live off of you for free. I don't like the way it makes me feel. This is my way of taking semi-control, or more like equal control in the relationship."

"Okay, deal." His relief was apparent.

"You thought I was going to break up with you, didn't you?"

"I wasn't sure, but I'll admit the thought of it scared the hell out of me."

"It's only been a day. I'd at least give you a week," I teased.

He laughed, putting his hands on my hips.

"A whole week, huh? That's very generous of you, I appreciate that."

Tilting his head down to mine he kissed me once, then again. I gave him a playful push backward as he came in for a third.

"You have work to do, Damon," I reminded him with a smile. "I'll be in the library."

I opened the LSAT book we'd gotten at the bookstore. I read the entire first chapter, doing the comprehension and quiz questions after each section. The memories of helping my father came back, as things I read reminded me of situations we'd been in together. Around lunch, I walked into the kitchen to make something. I popped my head into Damon's office again seeing him working on his computer.

"Day, do you want me to make you something for lunch?"

"Did you just call me Day?"

I blushed, admitting, "Yeah...I guess it just kind of came out. I don't have to call you that again if you don't like it."

He shook his head with a smile, "I love it and if you are making something, sure. If not, don't worry about it."

I made lunch for us both and brought it to him, munching on one of the sandwiches. His hand ran up the back of my thigh to rest on the small of my back.

"Thank you, beautiful."

I giggled, "Welcome."

I went back to studying, feeling better each time I turned the page.

The next morning, I walked downstairs and made a coffee for each of us. When I came back upstairs, Damon was awake and he took the coffee I offered him as I climbed back into my spot. His bare chest was on display and I saw a dip in his tattoo. I reached out to run my fingers over it.

"Is that a scar or a birthmark?" I asked, then blushed. "You don't have to answer that."

He smiled. "It's a scar." I chewed on my lower lip to prevent from asking more questions. It was too late to disguise my expression though. He'd seen it. "My ex-girlfriend gave it to me."

My jaw dropped. "Why?"

"Because I broke up with her. She was a little crazy."

"A little? Is that why you broke up with her?"

"No, I figured out that she wanted to be with me for my money."

I smiled mischievously. "Note to self: Don't let him figure out that you're stealing all his money."

He laughed. "I knew it."

My fingers traced it again, seeing his skin prickle with goosebumps. He put his hand under my chin, pulling me in for a kiss.

"I'm fine," he said, smiling. "Much better now."

I laughed, "Okay, Romeo, I have to get studying."

I felt his eyes following me as I walked out. He brought in breakfast not long after. I was in the middle of a problem on the quiz, lost in thought, my hair up in a messy bun as it helped me concentrate. He didn't say anything, just sat the plate next to me and walked out. When I finished, I looked at the plate, smiling. It was chocolate chip waffles. I dug in, not caring to read another word until I was done.

Chapter **Twenty**

I STUDIED NON-STOP, SCHEDULING TO TAKE MY TEST two weeks from the next day. Damon had brought me lunch and I was starting to feel the afternoon slump. I thought taking a power nap might help. I curled up on the couch in the library, letting my eyelids fall shut. A quick nap, I thought to myself. Then right back to studying.

I woke up feeling someone shake my arm lightly. Opening my eyes, I saw Max squatting in front of me.

"Max!" I smiled, reaching out to hug him.

He laughed, "Hey."

I got up, stretching, and saw Damon standing in the doorway with another man. They came in, and sat across from me. Max motioned for me to sit down, joining me.

"This is Mr. Garcia. He's the prosecutor for Austin's trial. He needs to talk to you," Max explained.

"Okay," I replied.

He stayed for an hour, asking me to recall what happened and how Austin treated me before I'd gotten away from him. Damon got me some water while Max grabbed tissues as I cried through my explanations.

"Noelle, it would really help if we had pictures of the scars Austin gave you. They would have to be taken by a medical doctor. You can set up an appointment with the doctor we normally work with. I can give you his number."

I leaned back on the couch, holding myself like it would shield me from what was to come. My eyes drifted across the library, to the shelf where my elephant sculpture now sat, proudly, confidently overlooking the room. I breathed in deeply, trying to draw in some of its courage.

"How much would it help?" I asked. "I mean, do I have to? You already have so much evidence from everything else that happened."

"Every bit of evidence helps. It will help build the case against him and it will give the jurors a visual so they can—"

"—better understand what I went through, I know," I nodded. "I'll take the doctor's number."

He wrote it down on a card, sliding it across the coffee table between us. We discussed our next meeting, as I was a key witness and had to testify against Austin.

"I'm going to ride back with Mr. Garcia to the city, but I'll be over later tonight," Max reassured me before leaving.

"Are you okay?" Damon asked as he came back to sit beside me.

"Yeah...I have to do this." I looked at him. "Will you be there? In the courtroom?"

"I will be there every step of the way." He kissed my temple.

Grace and Giovanni came over late in the afternoon and we fired up the grill. Damon passed grilling duties over to Grace, and we decided to take a dip in the pool. I was wearing a new bathing suit and Damon spent a lot of time telling me how nice I looked. Seeing how he gazed at me, I was starting to feel that I truly was beautiful. Max arrived just in time to help finish up on the grill.

"Day, will you hand me a towel?"

He reached over, and tossed it my way. Grace gave me a smirk.

"'Day', huh?"

I blushed. "It just happened."

"Mmm-hmm," she giggled. "Cute."

It felt normal to have a cookout. With Max there, it brought me back to the cookouts we used to have before I met Austin— ones filled with friends and family. I didn't have my parents there, but I had the rest of the important people in my life. Especially when Stefano and his wife came over to join us. I had a new family around me, one that I was slowly becoming a part of. It had been a long time since I felt like I belonged. No one could replace my parents, but even though they weren't physically there with me, I knew they were watching over us all.

Stefano and his wife stood.

"All right, kids, we're turning in for the night so you can get your actual celebration started," he smiled.

"What are you talking about?" Giovanni smiled.

"Oh, Gio, I was young once and I am no fool. I know the moment we leave Grace is going to bring out something to get you wasted." He patted his son on the back of the shoulder. "Nice try though."

Grace giggled, "Have a good night!"

Stefano gave us a wave. We sat around the fire, laughing and sharing stories. It was perfect. Grace got up and just as Stefano had predicted, brought out a large bottle of tequila. She poured shots, passing one to each of us before raising her glass in a toast.

"I just want to say, I'm glad Damon finally made it official with Noelle."

He laughed, kissing my cheek. "Me, too."

"I want to say something, too," I smiled, taking a deep breath. "It's been a long time since I have felt this much love and friendship," I began. "I want to say thanks for sticking by me through everything. I don't think I would have made it out without all of you. I want to toast to taking on whatever adventures the future holds, with great friends and a whole lot of love." I smiled as we clinked out glasses. "Oh, and for Max to finally find a girlfriend."

Gio shouted, "Cin cin!"

Max rolled his eyes dramatically, laughing as we took the shots.

Damon whispered in my ear, "Salute, my love."

"Cheers," I replied.

He held me tight, pouring his warmth into me with his

embrace. I knew the trial was coming, but I also knew I was stronger than I was before. It was like my final time to face Austin before he was put away for what he'd done. I had no idea what the future held for us after that, but I welcomed it with open arms.

9 798985 426212